Please return this book on or before the date shown above. To
renew go to www.essex.gov.uk/libraries, ring 0845 603 7628 or
go to any Essex library.

Essex County Council

'Our next date?' Rose said, her face flushing. 'But this isn't a date, is it? Just two friends out together.'

'Is that what you really think?' Jonathan said. 'Come on, Rose, pretending doesn't suit you. You and I both know that there's more to it than that. I want to get to know the real Rose Taylor, and I suspect you're not immune to me either.'

She raised her face to look him directly in the eye. 'We both know that we can't have a relationship,' she said flatly.

'Why not?' he asked.

She looked back at him. 'You know why not,' she said steadily.

'I'm not sure I do. I promise I'll be the perfect gentleman. Come on, what do you say?' He dropped his voice. 'Have a little fun.'

The thought took her breath away. This wasn't supposed to happen. This wasn't part of her plan. But if she couldn't offer him a future—well, neither was he suggesting one. She held out her hand. He looked at her in surprise before enveloping it in his. His hand was cool in hers, his long fingers that of a surgeon. A thrill ran up her spine. More than anything else in the world she wanted to know what it would feel like to be held in his arms. To have his mouth pressing down on hers. To lose herself in him—even if it was only for a short time.

Anne Fraser was born in Scotland, but brought up in South Africa. After she left school she returned to the birthplace of her parents, the remote Western Islands of Scotland. She left there to train as a nurse, before going on to university to study English Literature. After the birth of her first child she and her doctor husband travelled the world, working in rural Africa, Australia and Northern Canada. Anne still works in the health sector. To relax, she enjoys spending time with her family, reading, walking and travelling.

Recent titles by the same author:

RESCUED: MOTHER AND BABY
MIRACLE: MARRIAGE REUNITED
SPANISH DOCTOR, PREGNANT MIDWIFE*
THE PLAYBOY DOCTOR'S SURPRISE PROPOSAL

The Brides of Penhally Bay

PRINCE CHARMING OF HARLEY STREET

BY
ANNE FRASER

First published in Great Britain 2010
Large Print edition 2011
Harlequin Mills & Boon Limited,
Eton House, 18-24 Paradise Road,
Richmond, Surrey TW9 1SR

© Anne Fraser 2010

ISBN: 978 0 263 21718 6

Printed and bound in Great Britain
by CPI Antony Rowe, Chippenham, Wiltshire

PRINCE CHARMING
OF HARLEY STREET

For Stewart—
Thanks for the idea and, as always,
your help and support.

CHAPTER ONE

ROSE whistled under her breath as she glanced around the reception area in the doctor's surgery. It was nothing like anything she had seen before. Instead of the usual hard plastic chairs, dog-eared magazines and dusty flower arrangements, there were deep leather armchairs, piles of glossy magazines and elaborate—she would even go as far to say ostentatious—flower arrangements. She sneezed as the pollen from the heavily scented lilies drifted up her nostrils. They were going to have to go. Otherwise she would spend her days behind the burled oak desk that was her station with a streaming nose.

Grabbing a tissue from the heavily disguised box on her table, she blew her nose loudly and pulled the list Mrs Smythe Jones, the receptionist—no, sorry, make that personal assistant—had left for her.

The writing was neat but cramped and Rose

had to peer at the closely written words to decipher them.

It was Dr Cavendish's schedule for the week, and it didn't look very onerous. Apart from seeing patients three mornings a week, there were two afternoons blocked off for home visits. That was it. Nothing else, unless he had a hospital commitment that wasn't noted on the schedule. It seemed that Dr Cavendish must be winding down, possibly getting close to retirement. A vision of an elderly man with silver hair, an aristocratic nose and possibly a pince-nez popped into Rose's head.

Apart from the schedule Mrs Smythe Jones had also helpfully detailed Dr Cavendish's likes and dislikes. Apparently these included a cup of coffee from the cafetière—not instant—black, no sugar, served in a china cup and saucer which Rose would find in the cupboard above the sink in the kitchen in the back, and a biscuit, plain digestive, in the cupboard to the left of the one holding the cups. Patients were also to be offered tea—loose tea only, served in a teapot—on a tray, bottom-right cupboard, coffee, or bottled water, sparkling or still, from the fridge.

Looking at the schedule, it seemed that the first patient, an L. S. Hilton, wasn't due to arrive until 9.30. Plenty of time for Rose to have a good look around in advance. The cleaner, who had let Rose in a few minutes earlier, had disappeared, although she could hear the sound of a vacuum cleaner coming from somewhere further back.

There appeared to be two consulting rooms. Each of them bigger than most sitting rooms Rose had ever been in and almost identical to each other. There was the usual examination couch and screen, a sink, a desk and two armchairs, as well as a two-seater sofa in the corner by the window. There were landscapes on the wall, traditional in one of the rooms but modern brightly painted ones in the other, slightly out of sync with the antique furnishings of the room.

Rose stepped across to study the pictures more closely. Whoever had painted them had a sure eye and a love of colour. Like the pictures in the other room, these were also landscapes, but that's where the similarity stopped. Unlike the sedate country images next door, these were painted in sure, bold brushstrokes and depicted wild, stormy scenes which spoke to Rose of passion and loss. Whoever had picked them for the wall was someone with unconventional taste.

A polite cough behind her made her whirl around. Standing by the door was a man in his late twenties dressed formally in a suit and tie with black shoes polished to within an inch of their lives. He had light brown hair that was worn slightly too long and fell across his forehead. His face was narrow, his nose straight, and startling green eyes were framed by dark brows. But it was his mouth that caught Rose's attention. It was wide and turned up at the corners as if this was a mouth that was used to laughing.

'I'm sorry,' she apologised. 'You must be here to see the doctor. I didn't hear you come in.' For the life of her she couldn't remember the name of the first patient, only that it reminded her of a famous hotel chain.

'And you are?' The words were softly spoken with just the merest hint of bemusement.

'I'm Rose Taylor, the temporary receptionist.' She stepped back towards the door but the man stayed where he was, blocking her path.

'Where's Tiggy?' he asked. 'I mean Mrs Smythe Jones.'

'Mrs Smythe Jones is on leave. Now, if you wouldn't mind taking a seat in the waiting room, I'll just get your notes out.'

'Take a seat? In the waiting room? My notes.' The smile widened. 'I see. I don't suppose there's any chance of a cup of coffee while I'm waiting?'

'Of course,' Rose replied smoothly. 'I'll just pop the kettle on.'

When she came back from the kitchen, carrying a tray and trying not to feel too much like a waitress, he was sitting in her chair, leaning back with his arms behind his neck and his long legs propped on her desk.

'Excuse me, sir,' she said as politely as she could manage through gritted teeth. 'I think we agreed you'd take a seat in the waiting room.' He was beginning to annoy her. The way he was behaving as if he owned the place. However, on her first day she didn't want to cause a fuss. She needed this job. It paid well, extremely well paid, in fact, and the hours were flexible enough to give her time to help look after Dad. Perhaps this was the way all Harley

Street patients behaved. How was she to know? Nevertheless, it was unacceptably rude of him to put her in this position. What if Dr Cavendish walked in to find she had allowed a patient to take over her desk? She couldn't imagine him being best pleased.

The man jumped to his feet and took the tray from her hands. 'Please let me,' he said, laying the tray down on the desk. He looked at the single cup and saucer and raised an enquiring eyebrow. 'What about you? Aren't you joining me?'

Rose forced a polite smile. 'No, thanks.' She slid behind her desk before he could reclaim her chair. 'Now, what did you say your name was?'

'Jonathan.' He stretched out a hand. 'Jonathan Cavendish.'

'You're related to Dr Cavendish?'

The smile grew wider. 'I *am* Dr Cavendish.'

Rose was aware her mouth had fallen open. She quickly closed it.

'But you're young,' she protested, feeling her cheeks grow warm. What an imbecilic thing to say.

He looked puzzled. 'Twenty-seven, since you

ask. How old are you?' He leaned towards her and lazy eyes swept over her. 'No, don't tell me. Twenty-five?'

'Twenty-six, actually,' Rose conceded reluctantly. He was laughing at her, making her flustered. And she didn't do flustered. 'My name's Rose Taylor. The agency sent me over. To fill in until your usual receptionist returns.'

'Where did you say Mrs Smythe Jones was? I'm sure she didn't say anything about going on holiday.'

'I don't think it was a holiday.' Didn't this man know anything about the woman who worked for him? 'She had an emergency to do with her sister apparently. She called the agency on Friday, to ask for a temp.'

Jonathan frowned. 'I knew her sister hadn't been well. I was away this weekend, skiing. Couldn't get a signal on my phone—you know how it is.' He pulled his mobile out of his pocket. 'Still no message. I'll phone her later, after I've seen my patients.' He snapped the phone shut.

'Okay, so now we've that sorted, let's move on. Who's the first patient?'

Rose was still reeling from the discovery that this man was the doctor. Where was the elderly silver-haired man of her imagination? She was rapidly trying to process this new information. But it wasn't making any kind of sense.

As if he'd read her mind, Jonathan said, 'There is another Dr Cavendish, my uncle. But he retired last year. I took over the practice from him.'

Still confused, Rose studied the list in front of her. 'You have three patients this morning.' Only three! And each of them had been given half-hour slots. Half-hour slots! In the practice where she normally worked, the patients were lucky to get ten minutes with the overworked and harassed medical team. Either Dr Cavendish wasn't very good and no one wanted to come and see him, or he didn't like to work too hard. But it was none of her business how he ran his practice. 'And then you have a couple of home visits this afternoon. That's all Mrs Smythe Jones has marked down for you, unless there's another list somewhere?' Come to think of it, perhaps that was the answer?

She glanced around the desk. No, apart from this ornate leather-bound appointment book there was nothing else with information on it. Her eyes came to rest on the computer. That was it. There must be a computerised patient list. She stopped herself from smacking her head at her stupidity. Of course there would be a full list on the computer! The patients Mrs Smythe Jones had marked down in her neat hand must be additions.

Rose smiled apologetically at Jonathan, who was waiting patiently for a response, and booted up the hard drive. There had to be a password here somewhere.

'Oh, I'm sorry,' she apologised as the computer hummed into life. 'That must be the add-on list. As soon as I can get into the clinic on the computer, I'll be able to tell you who else is down for your clinic.'

The half-smile was back. 'You won't find anything on there. Mrs Smythe Jones doesn't believe in computers, I'm afraid. She uses it for letters, but that's it. The list you have in front of you is it.' He stood and straightened his already immaculately tied tie. 'Three patients sounds about right.' He held out his hand for the book. 'When the first patient arrives, just press this buzzer here.' He leaned back over the desk and Rose caught the scent of expensive after-shave. He straightened and pointed to a set of oak filing cabinets. 'Notes are in there. Now, if you'll excuse me. Vicki, my nurse, should be in shortly—she'll keep you right.' Without waiting for a reply, he retreated into the consulting room and closed the door behind him.

The first patient wasn't due to arrive for another half an hour. The cleaner came in and picked up the tray from the desk.

'His Lordship in, then? I'm Gladys by the way,' she said.

It was getting more confusing by the minute. His Lordship? Who the hell was she referring to? Did she mean Jonathan? In which case, it wasn't a very respectable way to speak about her boss.

Gladys chuckled. 'You haven't a clue what I'm talking about, dearie. Do you? His Lordship? Jonathan? The Honourable Jonathan Cavendish?'

Oh, my word. She was working for aristocracy.

Speechless, Rose could only indicate the closed door of the consulting room with a tip of her head.

'That's me, then, luvvie,' Gladys was shrugging into her coat. 'I'll get myself away home. Nurse will be in in a minute. I'll see you tomorrow. Ta-ra.'

Rose sat at the desk, completely stupefied. When a harassed staff member from the agency had rung her late on Friday afternoon, she'd been only too glad to get a job for the next few weeks. She hadn't stopped to ask about the practice, and even if she had wanted to, the voice on the other end of the line had made it clear she was in a rush.

'It's a minimum of four weeks, more likely five. Harley Street. Please say you can do it. They're new clients and we really want to keep them on our books. It involves the usual medical secretary work, plus manning the reception with possibly a bit of chaperoning thrown in. It'll be a piece of cake for someone with your experience.'

It had sounded right up Rose's street. Ever since Dad had had a stroke she'd known she would have to put her job in Edinburgh on hold and go and help her mother. Her parents hadn't wanted her to come home to London, but to Rose there had been no choice. Happily the practice she worked for as a practice nurse had been sympathetic and agreed to give her five weeks' leave, more if she needed it. The next few weeks would give her time to assess the situation at home and decide whether she should return to London permanently.

Harley Street was a couple of tube journeys away from her parents' house and meant an hour's commute at either end of the day, but it was a job and Rose had snatched the opportunity with both hands. Now she was wondering if she'd done the right thing. Then again, she hadn't much choice. There weren't that many temping jobs and she needed the money. Whatever reservations she might have about her new boss, the job was perfect.

She sighed and helped herself to another chocolate in the bowl on the desk. She let the rich flavours roll around her mouth. Delicious.

The door opened and an older woman with neatly coiffed hair and a small dog tucked under her arm swept into the room. Rose glanced at her sheet. Could this be L. S. Hilton?

'Such a naughty boy,' Mrs Hilton clucked. 'Snapping at that poor man's ankles. If you do that again, Mummy will get really angry with you.' Before Rose could react, she thrust the dog into Rose's arms. He was wearing a little coat that covered his legs and a scarlet ribbon in the hair on his head. 'Could you find him some chocolates? He always gets grumpy when his blood sugar gets low.' Then she peered at Rose over her spectacles. 'Oh, I don't think we've met, dear. Where is Tiggy?' She glanced around the room as if she might find her hiding somewhere.

'She's had to go away for a bit,' Rose said. The dog looked up at her with a distinctly unimpressed air. Rose was worried that he'd take a snap at her and she looked him firmly in the eye. She was used to dogs. Her parents had always had one when she had been growing up. You had to show them who was boss straight away. The dog whimpered and relaxed in her arms. She looked over to the desk for the chocolates. Her cheeks burned as she realised that she'd scoffed the lot. She should have known better than to leave the bowl in a place where her fingers could wander of their own accord. To her huge relief, Mrs Hilton didn't seem to notice the now empty bowl.

'Mr Chips likes you,' Mrs Hilton said approvingly. 'He doesn't usually take to strangers. And certainly not when he's grumpy.'

'If you could just take a seat, Mrs Hilton, I'll let the doctor know you're here. Then I'll see what I can find for Mr Chips. Can I get you something? A cup of tea, coffee?'

Mrs Hilton sat down on one of the chairs and picked up a magazine. 'No, thank you. Too much caffeine isn't good for my arthritis and...' she eyed Rose severely '...don't you know it's terribly bad for the skin? Like chocolates.' Her eyes flickered to the empty bowl and Rose felt her cheeks grow warmer. 'Although it seems you have good skin. Good girl. Most girls don't think about their skin until they reach my age and by then it's far too late to do anything about it. At least—' her eyes twinkled '—without the expertise of a good surgeon.'

Rose couldn't work out whether she was annoyed or flattered by Mrs Hilton's personal comments. But the gleam in older woman's eye made her go with the latter. She meant no harm.

Rose buzzed through to Jonathan to let him know Mrs Hilton had arrived.

'It's Lady Hilton,' he corrected mildly. 'I'll come out.'

The door opened almost before Rose had time to replace the handset. Jonathan paused in the door way and his mouth twitched as he noticed Rose trying to juggle Mr Chips with one arm while she searched for Mrs Hilton's notes with the other.

'Sophia,' he said, striding towards the older woman. 'How lovely to see you.'

Lady Hilton raised her face to his and Jonathan kissed her on both cheeks.

'You know I would have come to the house to see you? It would have saved you a journey into town,' he said.

'I had to come in anyway. I needed to do some shopping. And I wanted to talk to you about Giles—away from the house. He doesn't know I've been feeling poorly. And…' she looked at Jonathan sternly '…he's not to know.'

'Sophia, everything that you tell me is always in complete confidence,' Jonathan said firmly. He placed an arm under her elbow and without appearing to add any pressure, eased her to her feet. Despite the look of resolve on the older woman's face, Rose could tell the movement caused her some discomfort. Probably arthritis. Or something like it.

'Do you mind awfully keeping Mr Chips while I'm in with the doctor? He gets so restless if I don't pay him my full attention,' Lady Hilton asked Rose.

It wasn't really a question. Dog-sitting hadn't been in the job description. But, hey, it wasn't as if she was overrun with work, and he seemed to have gone to sleep in her arms.

Rose smiled. 'Don't worry. He'll be fine with me. If he wakes up and starts looking for you, I'll bring him in.'

While Rose waited for the next patient to arrive, she looked around for something to do. She liked to keep busy. Not that she could do much with a dog asleep in her arms. Spotting her discarded cardigan hanging on the back of the chair, she used one hand to form it into a little bed on the floor under her desk. She placed the sleeping dog on top. He looked at her with one eye, then gave a contented sigh and settled back down to sleep. Okay, what next? Perhaps she should ask Jonathan whether he would mind if she brought in some textbooks and did some revision in between patients? She couldn't see why he'd object. Unless she had more to occupy her, she'd go mad with boredom.

Her glance fell on the pile of magazines Lady Hilton had picked up in the short time she'd been in the waiting room. They were a mix of high-fashion glossies and society-gossip magazines, the type Rose never ever looked through—or at least never bought. She had to admit taking a sneaky look once or twice when she was at the hairdressers, but that wasn't the same as buying them. Other people's lives didn't really inter-est her, not unless they were doing something remarkable, like climbing Everest or walking unaccompanied to the South Pole. Now, those were people with intriguing lives, not folk who were famous, well, because they were married to a footballer or had a rich father.

Casually she flicked through the first maga-zine she picked up, curious despite herself. She came to a few pages near the middle, which had photographs of celebrities out on the town. Suddenly she stopped. Staring out at her, his arm around the waist of a woman with long wavy red hair, a figure to die for and a dress that would have cost Rose a year's salary, was Jonathan. He was dressed in a dinner jacket and a white shirt and appeared relaxed and at ease. Rose peered closer. Although he was smiling, there was something in his eyes that suggested he wasn't best pleased to be photographed. The caption underneath read 'The Honourable Jonathan Cavendish and his girlfriend, actress Jessamine Goldsmith, at the premiere of her film *One Night In Heaven.*'

Rose was having a hard time getting her head around it. He was an honourable, the son of a lord, his girlfriend was a movie star. And he was her boss. A GP. She felt her lips curl in disapproval. That wasn't the kind of doctor she approved of. People should go into medicine to help others, not to finance some gad-about lifestyle. However, it was nothing to do with her. She was here to do a job and as long as her new boss didn't actually go around killing his patients with his incompetence, who was she to judge?

The door swished open and she dropped the magazine as if it were a hot potato.

A woman with short curly hair and a look of panic rushed into the room. She ran past Rose without saying anything, heading straight for the staff bathroom. Once again, Rose was bemused. It was beginning to feel as if she had walked in to a madhouse. Who on earth was that? She hadn't rung the doorbell so she must have a key. And she knew exactly where the staff bathroom was. Could this be the missing Nurse Vicki?

A few minutes later, the woman reappeared. Although she still looked pale, some colour had returned to her cheeks.

'I'm so sorry,' she said collapsing into a chair. 'You must be the temp covering for Tiggy. She phoned me on Saturday to let me know she was going to be away and there would be a temp filling in.' She took a shuddering breath. 'You must think me incredibly rude, rushing in like that without so much as a good morning.'

Rose crossed to the woman's side. 'Are you all right?'

'Not really.' She grimaced before holding out a hand to Rose. 'I'm Victoria, my friends call me Vicki. I've just been terribly sick. Thank God I made it here in time. It would have been too embarrassing throwing up in public.'

'Should you be at work?' Rose said. 'Couldn't you have taken the day off?'

'I would have. If I hadn't known Tiggy was

off. Or if I'd known I was going to feel this bad. I felt okay until I got off the tube, then I just started to feel worse and worse.'

'Dr Cavendish is in with a patient. Should I call him?' Vicki did look awful. There was no way she should stay at work. Rose watched in alarm as the colour drained from the nurse's cheeks again.

'Oh, no, sorry.' Vicki clamped a hand across her mouth and bolted for the bathroom.

While she waited for Vicki to re-emerge, Rose switched the kettle on again and finding some peppermint tea set about making a pot. She hoped the drink would help settle Vicki's stomach. There was no way she could be allowed to return home until she stopped feeling ill.

'You must wonder what kind of place you've walked into.' Vicki's voice came from behind her. 'The nurse more ill than the patients. And I see Lady Hilton has brought Mr Chips in again. I do hope he won't relieve himself in the plant pot again. Oh, is that tea? Could I have some?'

'I think you should try a couple of sips. Why don't you sit down? You look as if you could collapse at any minute.'

Vicki sat on one of the chairs at the kitchen table. 'Jonathan is not going to be happy about this,' she confided. 'The last time I was off the full eight months. He had to find someone to replace me, and she didn't turn out to be great.'

Realisation was beginning to dawn on Rose. 'You're pregnant?'

Vicki nodded. 'Oh, I'd better not do that again,' she moaned. 'Any movement just makes it worse.'

'And you had hyperemesis with the last pregnancy.'

'Hey, you're pretty switched on. Have you had it? Is that how you know?' She was too polite to say so, but Rose guessed she was wondering how a medical secretary would know about the condition an unfortunate few women suffered in pregnancy.

'I'm a trained nurse. Poor you. How badly did you have it last time?'

'Bad enough to put me in hospital, I'm afraid. And to keep me off work for most of my pregnancy.' She took a tentative sip of her tea. 'I'm dreading having to tell Jonathan.'

'He doesn't know you're pregnant?'

'I wasn't going to tell him just yet. I'm only

eight weeks. And I hoped that I would be better this time around.'

'I'm sure he'll understand.'

'He's a real softy. Of course he'll understand. I just hate letting him down. The patients like to see me. They're used to me. Most of the older ones hate change. My obstetrician tells me it might get better by around twelve weeks, but I'm not holding my breath.'

The sound of a door opening alerted Rose to the fact that Jonathan's consultation with Lady Hilton had ended.

'I'll be back in a moment,' she reassured Vicki. 'Just you stay there until I get back.'

She scooped up Mr Chips from his nest in her cardigan and carried him over to Lady Hilton. The movement roused the dog from his nap and he reached up, attempting to lick Rose's face. She just managed to avert the doggy kiss by passing Mr Chips over to his owner.

'Has my baby been a good boy, then?' Lady Hilton cuddled her dog as if it had been days rather than minutes since they'd been together. But as she buried her face in her pet's fur, Rose noticed tears in the corner of her eyes.

'I'll come to the house to see you and Giles

later this week,' Jonathan said. 'In the mean-time, we'll try this new prescription. See if that makes a difference.' He patted her arm. 'The next few weeks are going to be rough,' he said. 'Call me any time. I mean it.'

He looked around. 'Rose, have you seen Vicki? She's usually in by now.'

'In the kitchen, having a cup of tea. I'm afraid she's not feeling very well.'

A look of concern swept across Jonathan's face. 'I'll go and check up on her. I'll see you soon, Sophia. Take care.' He kissed the woman on the cheek again and Rose showed her out.

Rose retreated behind her desk, giving Vicki the chance to tell Jonathan her news. She ran through the condition in her mind. Although hy-peremesis was hugely debilitating, it was rarely life threatening. However, being constantly sick would prevent Vicki from working and might well require another stay in hospital.

Jonathan appeared with his arm around Vicki's shoulder. 'I'm going to take Vicki home,' he said. 'Do you think you could hold the fort until I come back? I'll be about an hour.'

'Your next patient is due in about ten minutes,' Rose reminded him. 'Lord Bletchley?'

'I can manage, Jonathan,' Vicki said weakly. 'I'll take a taxi. You stay and see your patient. You know what Lord Wretchley—I mean, Lord Bletchley's like. He'll go through the roof if he's kept waiting.'

'He'll just have to,' Jonathan replied, looking determined. 'I don't want you to go in a taxi. Not when you might throw up again. You know what some of these drivers are like. They might well kick you out.'

'Couldn't I take your car and drive Vicki home?' Rose offered. 'My insurance allows me to drive any car. That way you could see Lord Bletchley on time. It does mean there wouldn't be anyone to cover reception, but seeing as it's only the one patient we're expecting, that shouldn't be too much of a problem. You can man the desk, whereas I'm not too sure he'd like to be seen by me.'

Jonathan smiled and Rose's heart gave a little blip. No man should have a smile like that, she thought. It just wasn't fair on women.

'Despite what anyone may have told you, I'm perfectly capable of answering the door.' He dug in his pocket. 'If you're sure you don't mind? My car's parked outside. Vicki knows which one it is.' He tossed a set of keys to Rose. 'It has satellite navigation so you should be able to find your way to Vicki's house and back okay.'

Ignoring Vicki's protests that really she could manage by herself, Rose retrieved a sick bowl from the treatment room and ushered her out the door.

'Okay, which one is his?'

Vicki pointed at a low-slung sports car. Rose felt the colour drain from her face. Although she knew relatively little about cars, she knew enough to know that the car must have cost at least as much as her parents' house. For a second, she was tempted to go back inside and tell Jonathan she had changed her mind. But one look at Vicki told her that she needed to be at home and in bed as soon as possible. If she put a scratch on the car, Little Lord Fauntleroy would just have to live with it.

Thankfully, Vicki knew how to work the sat nav and soon Rose was threading her way through the London traffic.

'You don't have to hold the steering-wheel as if it's a wild animal about to attack you,' Vicki said with a smile.

She was right. A child on a three-wheeler

would move faster. Rose forced herself to relax her grip. Now if only she could unclench her teeth, perhaps she could talk as well as drive.

But it seemed as if Vicki was no more capable of chatting than she was. The nurse leaned back against her seat and closed her eyes. Rose followed the instructions of the disembodied voice from the computer and by some miracle managed to find her way to Vicki's house without any disasters. Now all she had to do was make it back in one piece.

'Is there anyone at home to look after you?' she asked Vicki as they drew up in front of a small Victorian terrace.

'My husband,' Vicki replied. 'He's a police officer. He's on night duty so he'll be sleeping like the dead, but I'm sure he won't mind me waking him if I need anything. Our daughter is in nursery school.'

'I'll just see you safely in,' Rose said, and before Vicki could protest, she was out of the car and around the other side, helping her out.

Vicki smiled at her. 'Are you always this capable?' she said.

Rose smiled back. 'I can't help it. I was always the Guide who finished her badges long before anyone else did. The one who got the camp-fire going even when it was raining. It's social occasions that get to me. Doing is better than talking, if you know what I mean? Although I'm getting better at that. Needs must. In my other life I'm a nurse.'

Vicki frowned. 'Why are you covering for Tiggy as the receptionist? Oops, I mean personal assistant. That's how Tiggy prefers to be referred to. She's a sweetheart, but she thinks it's important everyone knows their place. Titles are important to her. And not just work ones either.'

'The job I was offered was as receptionist. I used to work as a medical secretary before I did my nurse training. I was happy to do either since I just wanted something short term.'

Vicki pulled a bunch of keys from her bag and opened her front door. 'I can manage from here,' she said. 'I'm sorry that you've had all this dumped on you on your first day. I hope we haven't scared you off. Johnny will need help. Would you be a sweetheart and phone the nursing agency and find out about a replacement for me?'

'Don't worry, I'll sort it out. You get to bed

and I'll see you whenever you come back to work.'

Vicki grimaced. 'God knows when that'll be. Jonathan made me promise not to come back until I've stopped being sick. If it follows the same pattern as last time, it could be months.'

'I'll speak to him about finding someone to cover for you as soon as I get back to the office.' Rose made her voice stern. 'Now, inside and off you go to bed.'

By the time Rose, with an enormous sigh of relief, returned to the surgery, it seemed as if Lord Bletchley had been and gone. Jonathan was back at her desk with his feet up, flicking through the magazine Rose had skimmed through earlier. He was scowling.

'Bloody paparazzi,' he muttered. 'Can never get their facts right.' He flung the magazine aside and got to his feet. 'How is Vicki?'

'She was going to go straight to bed. Her husband's on night duty, so he'll keep an eye on her.'

Jonathan pulled his hand through his thick dark hair. 'I can't see her being back for at least a month. If then. Would you mind getting onto the nursing agencies? You'll find the number of the one we use regularly in the diary. Ask if there's anyone who could cover on a day-to-day basis for the next four weeks at a minimum.'

An idea was beginning to form in Rose's head, but she liked to think things through before she spoke. Jonathan looked at his watch. 'I'll be in my room if you need me. I've a couple of phone calls to make.'

Could she? Should she? Rose rolled the idea around in her head. It would be the perfect solution. She was a trained nurse and there really wasn't that much to keep her busy at the desk. Mrs Smythe Jones had told her that she hoped to be back in a week or two. Rose could combine both roles for a short time. She'd much prefer to be kept busy. And if they needed someone to man the desk while she was in with a patient, she thought she had a solution to that too.

The ringing of the door interrupted her musings. She pressed the door release and watched bemused as a teenage boy with a resentful expression was almost dragged inside by an irate-looking woman.

'Come on, Richard,' the woman was saying. 'We might as well see the doctor now we're here.'

The boy looked at Rose through long hair that almost covered his face and Rose bit down the stab of sympathy that swept over her. He had the worst case of acne she had seen outside a textbook. His face was covered with angry raised bumps and he looked utterly miserable. Underneath the bad skin, Rose could see that he could be a good-looking boy, if it weren't for the surly expression and terrible acne. It brought back memories of her own teenage years, when she had felt as self-conscious with her height as this boy clearly did with his skin.

She smiled at the boy, knowing how embarrassed he would be feeling.

'You must be Richard Pearson,' she said. 'If you want to take a seat with your mother, I'll let the doctor know you're here.'

All Rose got in reply was a grunt. Nevertheless he sat down, dipping his head so his hair covered his face.

His mother looked at him with a mixture of frustration and love. 'I apologise for my son's rudeness,' she said. 'He didn't want to come.' She turned her back to her son, leaned across the desk and continued, her voice lowered to a whisper, 'I'm at my wits' end. He's refusing to go to school now. He just sits in his room, playing on his computer. I've tried other doctors. Dr Cavendish is my last hope. I heard from a friend that he helped her daughter.' She glanced behind her again. Richard was engrossed with his mobile; either playing a game or texting.

'I'm sure Dr Cavendish will do everything he can. I'll just let him know you're here.' Rose certainly hoped he could help. Nothing so far had given her any confidence in his medical ability. Oh, he was certainly charming. The way he had been with Lady Hilton had made that evident, but no amount of charm was going to help this poor unhappy boy. At the very least surely he would refer him to a dermatologist?

She buzzed through. 'I have Richard Pearson to see you,' she said.

'I'll be right out.' He really did have a lovely voice. Deep with just a hint of a Scottish accent.

As before, he was out of his room almost before she had a chance to put the phone down. He went over to the boy and held out his hand. 'I'm Dr Cavendish. But you can call me Jonathan, if you like. Why don't you come into my room and we can have a chat?'

Richard reluctantly got to his feet, and scowled at his mother.

Something in his expression must have caught Jonathan's attention. 'Why don't you stay here, Mrs Pearson?' he said, his voice as smooth as silk. 'And have a cup of tea while I talk to your son on his own for a bit. Then if you have any questions, I'll be happy to answer them.'

'I'd like to come in with my son,' Mrs Pearson said stubbornly.

Richard looked at his feet and shuffled them uncomfortably.

'Richard? What would you like? I see from your notes that you're seventeen so I'm happy to see you on your own. However, if you'd prefer your mother to come in with you, that's perfectly all right too.'

'On my own,' Richard mumbled with an apologetic look at his mother. 'I'll be okay, Mum. As the doctor says, I'm almost eighteen.'

Mrs Pearson seemed unconvinced. Rose touched her gently on the elbow.

'Why don't I get us both a cup of tea?'

Mrs Pearson watched Jonathan lead her son away, but then let Rose guide her over to one of the armchairs and sit her down.

'I don't really want any tea,' she said. 'I just want to get my son helped. This time last year he was popular and outgoing, and he seemed so happy. But ever since the problem with his skin, he's become so withdrawn and miserable. I keep telling him that it'll get better in time, but he says he doesn't care. It's now that matters.' She drew a shaky breath. 'I'm so scared he'll do something silly.'

Rose sat down next to the distraught mother. 'There are medicines that can help. It's often just a case of finding the right one. As soon as he knows we can improve his skin, he'll be happier. It's too cruel that he's been hit with this just at a time when his hormones are already all over the place.'

'I hope you're right.' The woman sniffed and then looked at Rose, puzzled. 'I guess you pick up all sorts of information working in a doctor's practice.'

'I guess you do.' Rose smiled. There was no point in telling her that she had spent the last four years studying nursing, and dermatology had been one of the last modules before she'd qualified. And as for understanding teenage angst, it hadn't been that long since she'd been through it herself. She remembered only too well how awful it felt to be the odd one out. Somehow at that age you could never accept that others had the same feelings of inadequacy and that they were just better at hiding it. Not that she could imagine Dr Jonathan Cavendish going through anything like it. She doubted that he'd had a moment's uncertainty about his looks in his life.

She chatted with Richard's mother until almost half an hour had passed. Eventually, Richard emerged with Jonathan. To her relief the teenager seemed much happier. He almost managed a smile for his mother.

'So take the tablets for a week and come back and see me. If things haven't improved substantially, we'll think of what to do next. One way or another, we'll get on top of this.'

Richard's mother looked uncomfortable for a moment. Rose guessed instantly that she might be worrying about the cost of the consultation and medication.

'Oh, and by the way, the follow-up consultations are included in the price of this appointment. I've also given Richard a letter to take to his GP, who'll be happy to give him the prescription on the NHS. I hope that's okay.'

There was no disguising Mrs Pearson's relief. Rose warmed to Jonathan. He had done that so gracefully she doubted Mrs Pearson or her son suspected for a moment that he was lying about the cost of the consultations. It was all there in the brochure she had read that morning. Thankfully, Mrs Smythe Jones had said on her detailed list that she'd catch up with the billing on her return. So many of their patients had different arrangements for payment that it would be far too complicated for a temp to work out who was to be billed what and when.

As soon as mother and son had left, Rose turned to Jonathan.

'What did you prescribe?'

He looked at her baffled. 'Amoxicillin. Why do you want to know?'

Rose felt her cheeks grow warm. She hadn't decided whether to tell him she was a nurse, but now it seemed as if she had no choice.

'I'm a trained nurse,' she admitted finally. 'A practice nurse, and I not too long ago completed a course on dermatology, so I kind of wondered what you thought you could do for him. I know topical retinoids can help when antibiotics don't.'

His frown deepened. 'A nurse? Why are you working as a...?' He stopped in mid-sentence.

Rose had to smile at his obvious discomfort. 'I'm on leave from my job for a few weeks for personal reasons. I was a medical secretary until five years ago, so I'm also qualified to do this job. When I was working as a medical secretary, I realised as I typed up the notes for the doctors that what I was reading really fascinated me and I wanted to know more.'

Oops. What was she doing? There was something in the way he was looking at her with those steady curious green eyes that was making her babble. And she was usually so reticent when it came to talking about herself.

He did look genuinely interested, although Rose had the strong suspicion that was just part of his practised charm. In which case, why on earth was she telling him? But she could hardly stop now. 'Anyway, my boss encouraged me to study for my A levels in my spare time and then apply to university, and they accepted me.' Try as she would, she couldn't quite prevent the note of pride creeping into her voice. She was the first person in her family who had gone to university and her parents had almost burst with pride.

'So why are you here?' He sounded puzzled. 'Why didn't you take a nursing job? God knows, this city is desperate for trained nurses.' His eyes were casually moving up and down her body, as if he were a cat and she the cream. She should have been annoyed, but she knew it couldn't be because he found her attractive. Not this man. Suddenly she regretted wearing her old interview suit and primly buttoned-up blouse. Nevertheless, there was something deliciously unexpected about the way it made her feel. For a second she almost forgot the question.

'Rose?' he prompted.

Now see what she had started. This was where she should tell him about her home situation and despite his interested gaze she wasn't sure he would really want to know.

'Go on,' he encouraged. 'I'd really like to know,' he said as if reading her mind. He leaned against the filing cabinets and folded his arms, his eyes never straying from her face.

'Let's just say family circumstances and leave

it at that?' She kept her voice light, but returned his stare directly. It really was none of his business. He was her boss but that didn't give him the right to give her the third degree. Okay, so it wasn't exactly the third degree, but it was more than she wanted to tell him.

He was still studying her intently and she could see the same thought processes going through his head as had gone through hers earlier. She was a nurse. He needed a nurse, and quickly.

'Did you have any luck with the agency? About a replacement for Vicki?' he asked.

'I haven't called yet,' she admitted. 'I was thinking…' She took a deep breath. What if he hated her suggestion? For all she knew, practices like this wanted their nurses to have the right kind of accent. The right kind of image. Although there was nothing wrong with the way she spoke, her voice didn't have the plummy ring to it that Vicki's voice did.

'That since you're a nurse, you could fill in for her? Exactly what I was thinking. But what about the office? I'm not sure you could do both jobs.'

Rose hid a smile. She could easily manage

both jobs if it were a simple case of workload, but he was right. There did need to be someone at the desk if she was in with a patient.

'I know just the person for the office,' she said. 'She's young, but keen. She's at a bit of a loose end while she's looking for a permanent job. I know she'll be glad to work any hours needed, but she also won't mind if you need to let her go at any time.'

'Cool. Can I leave you to sort it out? Tiggy always manages that side of things. I'm afraid I'm useless at anything except the medical side.' He glanced at his watch. 'Lunchtime! Where do you fancy eating?'

Rose gaped at him. There was no way she wanted to go to lunch with him. Not today, possibly never. She was having way too odd a reaction to him, and she wanted some time to examine what was happening. It had always worked in the past. Thinking about something logically made it easier to deal with. Besides, she had brought her own snack. She really couldn't afford to eat out.

'I brought a packed lunch,' she said primly. 'I'm quite happy to have it at my desk.'

His lips twitched, but he didn't try to persuade

her. He was probably relieved she had said no. No doubt it was his impeccable manners that had prompted his offer in the first place and no doubt he would have been mortified had she said yes. Somehow she guessed that the hired help going out with the boss wasn't the way things were done in this part of London.

Jonathan ran down the stairs of his London consulting rooms and into the frosty spring air. He couldn't help smiling when he thought of the temp. She was a lot better looking than Mrs Smythe Jones, that was for sure. Although he had a soft spot for the elderly receptionist, who had been there since he'd been in short trousers, he was looking forward to the next few weeks. Rose Taylor intrigued him. The baggy cardigan she was wearing couldn't quite disguise a figure that would make most of his female acquaintances weep into their champagne. Luckily he was a connoisseur of women though; anyone else would have failed to see that she was a stunner under that shapeless cardigan and old-fashioned glasses. And he'd liked the way she had dealt with his patients. Solicitous but not overbearing. He couldn't help but notice the way they responded to her. Even Lady Hilton, who usually was as narky as the dog she insisted carrying everywhere, had been like putty in her hands. She was the most intriguing woman he had met since—well, for a long time. The unusual mix of prickly personality, which reminded him of a teacher he'd had at school, and hidden sex appeal. How could a woman be sexy and sexless at the same time? He whistled as he made his way to the restaurant. It was going to be interesting having Rose Taylor around.

CHAPTER TWO

ROSE waited until the door had closed behind Jonathan before she let out her breath. She collapsed in the chair. He was gorgeous—and that smile! Did he have any idea what it did to women? Of course he did. Rose's experience of men was limited but even she recognised a man who was used to being admired. She had never met anyone like him. After all, how could she have? Those weren't the circles she moved in. But good looking though he was, she was not sure whether she approved of him. She much preferred men who had a sense of purpose, men who had some ambition, and taking over the family practice in order to have an easy life was as far off ambition as she could imagine. Not that she'd had many boyfriends. Three at the last count and none of them could be called exciting. But at least they were reliable. Reliable and safe. Somehow she knew safe wasn't a word that could be applied to Jonathan Cavendish.

And it was just as well she preferred sensible men, she thought ruefully. The chances of Jonathan Cavendish being interested in her were less than zero. All she had to do was look at that flame-haired bombshell in the picture with him. She was so perfect—there was no way she would be found absent-mindedly munching her way through a bowl of chocolates.

She glanced around the surgery. Enough of that sort of thinking. What now? He had left her his Dictaphone with his notes about the patients he had seen, so she could type them up and have them ready for him to sign on his return. And as for the rest of the afternoon? There were three home visits marked down in the book. What was she supposed to do while he was away? She swallowed a sigh. It was going to be a long day.

As she'd expected, it only took her thirty minutes to type up the letters on the computer. The note paper was as grand as the rest of the consulting rooms.

Just as she was preparing to eat her lunch, there was a frantic knocking on the door. She opened it to find a woman about her age with a young child of about two in her arms.

'Please,' she gasped. 'Is there a doctor around? My daughter's having difficulty breathing. I don't know what happened—one minute she was okay then she started wheezing. My mobile's battery's flat or else I would have called an ambulance. Then I looked up and saw the doctor's name on the door. Please help me.'

Rose could see that the young mother wasn't far off hysteria. The little girl was having difficulty breathing but at least her lips were pink and the muscles in her neck weren't standing out with each breath. The little girl was clutching a teddy bear as if her life depended on it.

She gripped the woman's shoulder. 'I know it's difficult,' she said, 'but you have to calm down. Your little girl will get more distressed if she sees you panicking. Now what's her name?'

'Sally,' the woman replied after taking a couple of deep breaths. 'I'm Margaret.'

'Could she have choked on anything? Inhaled something? A button? A peanut? Anything?'

'Not as far as I know.'

'Sally, I'm just going to look inside your mouth. Okay?' Rose said calmly. The little girl looked at her with frightened eyes. Rose gently checked inside her mouth. There was nothing obvious blocking the little girl's throat. If there had been, her breathing would have been much noisier. It was still an emergency, but not one that was immediately life threatening.

'Okay, Margaret, come with me,' Rose said, taking the little girl from her mother's arms and walking briskly to the treatment room.

'I was just having a coffee in the café round the corner and she was fine then.' Margaret had calmed down a little, although anxiety and fear were still evident in her eyes.

'Has this happened before?' Rose asked. 'Any history of asthma or allergies?' There were two obvious possibilities as far as Rose could tell. Either Sally was having an asthma attack, in which case she needed a nebuliser, or she was having a severe allergic reaction, in which case she needed adrenaline. But which one was it?

'Could you open your mouth as wide as you can, Sally? I'm just going to shine a torch down your throat. It won't hurt at all, I promise.'

The little girl did as she was told. Rose shone the torch. As far as she could see, there was no swelling of the throat.

'Is it possible she's eaten a peanut? Or some other food she's not had before?'

The mother shook her head. 'She was in her high chair. All she had was the juice I gave her.'

In the background Rose heard the slamming of the door and then a voice calling her name. A wave of relief washed over her. It was Jonathan. At least now she'd have help.

'In the treatment room,' she called out. 'Could you come, please?'

He appeared at the door of the room and took the situation in at a glance. He crouched next to the chair where Rose had plonked Sally back on her mother's lap.

He touched the little girl lightly on the cheek. 'Hello, there,' he said softly. 'What's all this, then? You're having difficulty breathing?'

While he was talking to the girl, Rose had located a nebuliser and some liquid salbutamol. As he started to listen to the little girl's chest she held the vial up to him and he nodded approvingly towards her.

'Margaret, do you know how much Sally weighs?' Rose asked. 'It'll help us work out how much medicine to give her.'

'I'm not sure, maybe about twelve kilograms. I haven't weighed her recently. There's been no need.'

Now that Margaret knew her daughter was getting the help she needed, some of the terror had left her voice.

'It's okay. We can make an estimate.'

Rose reached for a pulse oximeter. 'I'm just going to put this on your toe,' she said to Sally. 'It won't hurt either. It's just a little toy I have to help me. Okay?' Rose turned to Margaret. 'It'll monitor Sally's blood oxygen levels. Tell us how much oxygen she's taking in.'

The child was still having problems with her breathing, but now that her mother had calmed down, some of the panic had subsided and her breathing was becoming easier. Nevertheless, she still needed treatment.

'I think your daughter is having an asthma attack,' Jonathan said, taking the nebuliser from Rose. 'I'm just going to put this over your mouth, Sally, and I want you to take slow, deep breaths.'

The little girl shook her head from side to side, the panic beginning to return.

Frantically Rose looked around then she had

an idea. She lifted the teddy from the little girl's arms and placed a second nebuliser over the toy bear's mouth. Rose crouched by Sally's side and, placing her hands on either side of the little face, forced her to look into her eyes.

'Watch me, Sally. We're going to play a game. Every time I take a breath, like this, Teddy's going to take a breath. You copy us, okay?

It seemed to work. Her eyes fixed on Rose and the teddy bear, Sally copied every breath Rose took. Jonathan watched carefully not saying anything. Slowly, Sally's breathing returned to normal and after a while Jonathan removed the mask from the little girl's face.

'Your breathing should be all right now, Sally.' He turned to her mother.

'This is the first time it's happened? Never before?'

Margaret shook her head.

'It probably didn't seem that way to you but I think that some of the problem was that Sally was getting quite panicky when she felt her breathing was tight. We could tell from looking at her breathing that she was still managing to take plenty of air into her lungs—her oxygen reading was ninety-eight per cent, which is pretty good, even when she was at her most distressed. Even so, it was a very scary experience for you both,' Jonathan explained.

Sally's mother looked weak with relief. The little girl hid her head in her mother's neck and closed her eyes. Rose knew that sleep would be the best thing for the child now.

'We had been to the park to feed the ducks with a friend. Sally was sleepy so she went for a nap in my friend's arms. When she woke up she needed to go to the bathroom, so I took the chance to have a coffee. She had been coughing in the park a little, but I didn't think anything of it. It was only when we were in the coffee shop that she seemed to have difficulty getting her breath. I thought she'd be better in the fresh air but she kept on getting worse. Then I saw the name on the door. I hoped there would be someone who could help.'

She looked at Jonathan and Rose, her eyes glistening. 'Thank you, both. I don't know what I would have done if you hadn't helped me.'

'I think it's Rose who deserves most of the thanks,' Jonathan said, straightening. He looked at her as if she puzzled him—as if she were a crossword and he was missing several clues.

'You should see your own doctor as soon as you can. I suspect Sally is going to need regular medication for a while,' he told Margaret.

Rose was turning over what Sally's mother had said.

'Do you have pets, Margaret?'

'No, we don't. Sally's dad is allergic to animal fur.'

'What about this friend? The one you met in the park?'

'Linda? Oh, yes. She has about five cats. She loves them and is always rescuing another one.'

Rose caught Jonathan's eye and knew he was thinking the same thing she was.

'I think we might have found the culprit. It's possible your daughter is allergic to cat fur. Perhaps there were cat hairs clinging to your friend and when Sally fell asleep in her arms she inhaled some of the allergens. Anyway, it's only a possibility, but one worth thinking about and mentioning to your GP when you see him,' he said.

Margaret refused a cup of tea, but accepted Rose's offer to call her a taxi. Ten minutes later she was climbing into the cab, her sleeping child in her arms, still thanking Jonathan and Rose effusively.

When they had left, Rose turned to Jonathan. 'I hope you're all right with me bringing them in. I realise it wasn't anything to do with your practice and if I had messed up, you could have been held liable.'

Jonathan looked at her his expression serious. 'And if I told you that it was unforgivable, that you have never to help a passer-by again, what would you say?'

'I would say that you need to find another temp,' Rose replied hotly, before she noticed that corners of his mouth had lifted in a smile. 'You're kidding, right?' she said, embarrassed she had jumped to the wrong conclusion so quickly.

'Of course I'm kidding,' he said. 'I wouldn't dream of employing someone who would think of rules before they acted. That wouldn't be right and...' his smile grew wider and Rose felt the strangest feeling in the pit of her stomach "...so boring.'

He levered himself away from the wall against which he'd been leaning. 'I think you've had enough excitement for the day. Why don't you do the letters from this morning and then get away home?'

'Letters are done, just waiting for your signature,' Rose replied. What on earth did he think she'd being doing while he'd been out to lunch? She glanced at her watch. 'It's only two o'clock. I can't possibly leave this early.'

He looked thoughtful.

'How would you like to come on a home visit with me, then? From what I saw back there, the way you dealt with Margaret and Sally, you'd be perfect to step in for Vicki. What do you say? It'll mean more money, of course.'

The nervous flutter in the pit of her stomach spread upwards. The look in his eyes was a heady mixture—sexy, naughty, mischievous. Rose had never felt so flustered in her life, but she was damned if she was going to let him see the effect he was having on her. She held out her hand. 'You have a deal. And if you're happy for me to find someone for the office, I can do that too. I'll write down a name and number so you can check my references.'

He raised his eyebrows at her before shaking her hand. 'Somehow I get the feeling they're going to be first class.'

Rose tried to ignore the warmth that was spreading through her body.

'Is it usual for you to take the office staff on a home visit?' she asked.

'Not really. But the visit I have down for the afternoon isn't the easiest.'

For the first time since she'd met him, he looked uncomfortable. 'It's to Jessamine Goldsmith's house.' She was the actress, the one who had been with him in the photograph in the magazine. His girlfriend.

'And let's just say that it would make me feel much more comfortable having you there.'

'Isn't she your girlfriend?' What on earth was Jonathan thinking? It was completely against the rules for a doctor to date a patient.

He narrowed his eyes at her. 'What makes you say that?'

Involuntarily, Rose's eyes slid to the magazine.

Jonathan's eyes followed hers. He looked none too pleased when he realised what she'd seen.

'Let's clear one thing up,' he said. 'Never ever believe what you see in these magazines. Jessamine Goldsmith is *not* my girlfriend and never has been. She's a patient who just happens to move in the same social circles as I do.'

'In which case...' Rose raised an eyebrow while hiding a smile '...what are we waiting for?'

As he manoeuvred the car through the thick London traffic, he flicked a switch and the rich sounds of Debussy filled the car. It was a composer Rose loved. She sat back in her seat, aware of the scent of expensive aftershave mingling with the smell of leather. It was so much better being in this car without having to drive. All she had to do now was relax.

'How come we're going to see Miss Goldsmith at home? Is she really unwell?'

Jonathan flicked her a smile.

'Jessamine's almost certainly fine, believe me. She simply prefers to have me see her at her house. A lot of the patients do. They find it less stressful.' Again there was the smile. 'Naturally, if they need to come to the consulting rooms for tests, then they do. Or if they're shopping nearby. Some, however, prefer me to come to them. It's much more discreet. Take Jessamine, for example, the press follow her everywhere, as they do many of my patients. Any visit to the doctor is viewed with curiosity and speculation. As you can imagine, most people prefer not to have that kind of conjecture in the public domain.'

'But aren't they equally curious about a visit from the doctor?'

At this point they had left the traffic behind and were driving through one of the more exclusive parts of London. Jonathan pulled up outside a house that could have been a hotel it was so large. The Victorian façade was the grandest she had ever seen. Two tall pillars framed a massive front door.

Jonathan turned off the ignition. 'Except that they can never be sure whether I'm visiting as a doctor or as a friend. Most of my patients belong to the same social circle as I do. You can't imagine how many off-the-record consultations I do at a party or at Ascot.'

All this was more and more confusing. Rose frowned.

'That can't be good. Surely there needs to be some distinction between the doctor and the patient?'

He jumped out of the car. 'Nope. It works just fine, believe me.'

The door was opened, before they had a

chance to knock, by a man dressed in a formal suit.

'Good afternoon, sir,' he said. 'And miss. Miss
Goldsmith is waiting for you in the drawing
room. She said I was to show you straight in.'

Rose wanted to giggle. It was like being
caught in a time warp. But if Jonathan found it
amusing, he gave no indication of it. Instead, he
stepped back to allow Rose to go through the
door in front of him.

She stepped into a hall, so enormous her parents' whole house could have easily fitted into
it—possibly twice. The floor was marble, paintings hung on the wall, and sculptures and large
vases holding extravagant flower arrangements
were placed around the space. To one side was
a fireplace and a small sofa.

'I know my way, thank you, Robert,' Jonathan
said, and taking Rose by the elbow steered her
across the hall and up a flight of stairs that
wouldn't have looked out of place in the foyer
of the grandest cruise ship. Everywhere Rose
looked there were ornate statues and gilt or-
naments. Although someone had lavished a
fortune on the interior, it wasn't to her taste.

Rose much preferred a minimalist, uncluttered look.

Inside another equally impressive room, almost hidden in the depths of a sofa, was a woman with fine features and a mass of red hair. As soon as she saw Jonathan, she jumped to her feet and came towards him, arms outstretched.

'I've been waiting all day for you to come.' She pouted, holding up her face to be kissed.

'I do have other patients, Jess,' Jonathan said, bending and kissing her on the cheek. 'I've brought someone with me. This is Rose Taylor, my…er…nurse for the next few weeks.'

Rose stood trying not to shuffle her feet like some sort of servant from the Middle Ages. She smiled and held out her hand. 'I'm pleased to meet you, Ms Goldsmith.'

Jessamine studied her for a second, her glance no doubt taking in the cheap suit Rose wore. Whatever she saw seemed to reassure her and she smiled, the famous smile Rose knew from the times she had seen her in the movies. It lit up her face, turning her from a petulant teenager into a woman of remarkable beauty.

Jessamine ignored Rose's outstretched hand

and dropped two air kisses on either side of Rose's cheeks.

'Would you like something to drink? Champagne perhaps? Tea?'

'Tea would be lovely,' Jonathan said firmly. 'Now, Jessamine, what can I do for you?'

'It's my stomach,' she said. 'It hurts like crazy.'

'Why don't you lie down while I take a look?' Jonathan suggested.

'Perhaps Rose wouldn't mind going downstairs to organise the tea while you're examining me?' There was no mistaking the glint in Jessamine's eye.

'Sorry, Jess, I need Rose here.' He sent Rose a look that implied that if she even thought about leaving him alone, she would have him to answer to. 'In case I need to take blood. Now, don't be difficult, let's have a look. Have you been eating properly? You know we spoke about this before. Your tummy hurts because you're hungry. You have to have more than five hundred calories a day.'

'That's all very well for you to say.' Jessamine pouted again. 'You know how the camera adds pounds and I have an audition tomorrow.'

Jessamine lay down on the sofa and lifted her T shirt, revealing her stomach. It was, as Rose had suspected, as flat as a pancake. But Jonathan was right, she was too thin. Rose could almost count each individual rib poking through the skin. When Jonathan made Jessamine sit up, so he could listen to her breathing from her back, it was the same, each vertebrae sticking out like a railway track.

'Your chest is fine and so is your heart. Rose, could you take Jessamine's blood pressure, please?'

It took Rose about two seconds to wrap the cuff around the too-thin arms. The blood pressure was slightly on the low side, but nothing particularly concerning. Despite her thinness, Jessamine was, on the surface, in good physical condition. While Rose was taking her blood pressure, Jessamine was talking to Jonathan. She was speaking too fast, her eyes bright and feverish.

'I hope you haven't forgotten about the Wakeleys' yacht party next weekend, Johnny? All the crowd is going. I know you and Felicity aren't together any more, but you mustn't stay at home and mope. You must come too, Rose,' she added as an afterthought.

Rose knew it was only politeness that had made Jessamine invite her.

'I'm sure Rose would love to come,' Jonathan said before Rose could decline. 'In fact, I'll bring her myself.'

The response was obviously not what Jessamine had been hoping for. She narrowed her cat's eyes at Rose, and then with another dismissive glance seemed to remember that Rose offered no competition.

Rose opened her mouth to protest. She might be working for Jonathan, but that didn't give him the right to accept invitations on her behalf. Besides, she had her own plans. She would be going down to the pub, her old local, to meet up with friends she hadn't seen for months. Nevertheless, she felt slightly wistful. When was the last time she'd been to a party? And when would she ever have a chance to go to one like the one Jessamine was talking about? Never was the answer. But there was no point in even thinking about it: she'd be completely out of her depth. She caught Jonathan's eye. He was looking at her, willing her not to contradict him, so she wouldn't. She could always send her apologies with him on the night.

Eventually, after Jonathan had taken some blood and given Jessamine a lecture about eating properly and had received a promise in return that everyone in the room knew was empty, he made their excuses.

'We'll see you a week on Sunday, Jess,' he said. 'And I'll come back and see you before then. I don't think there's anything to worry about at the moment, but I'm going to keep an eye on you. But you have to eat more regularly. If you don't, you will continue to suffer from indigestion. But that's not the only thing. You're harming your body by starving yourself.' He frowned down at her. 'Is it really worth putting your health at risk, Jess?'

'Please don't tell me off, Johnny. I promise I'll be good. I just have to audition for this next film and then I'll put a few pounds back on, I promise.'

She held up two fingers in a salute Rose knew well. 'Brownies' honour.' She slid a pointed glance at Rose. Her look was mocking and challenging at the same time. She had taken a dislike to Rose, that much was obvious, and Rose had no idea why.

Outside, Jonathan held open the door of his car. 'Can I drop you off at home?' he asked.

Rose shook her head. 'I think there's a tube station not far from here. I need to pick up a few things on my way home so, thanks, but no thanks.'

'Then I'll drop you off at the station. Hop in. We can have a chat about Jessamine on the way.'

Rose did as he suggested. 'You seemed pretty sure it was indigestion,' she said.

'I am. Given her lifestyle, it's the likely diagnosis. But I'm not ruling out other possibilities just yet either. I want to check her blood count—do a full blood screen, just to be on the safe side.'

Although it probably was just indigestion, Rose had been worried that Jonathan didn't seem to be taking the symptoms seriously enough. There was something about the casual way the consultations were held, the familiarity with the patients, that disturbed her. Jonathan's manner was so easygoing, her earlier doubts were resurfacing. Did he really know what he was doing? However nothing in the thorough way he examined the patients or his detailed notes suggested otherwise. Perhaps it was simply that this world was so different from anything she had ever encountered.

'You think it could be more than indigestion?' she asked.

'Let's just say I'm not going to take any chances.'

Rose was relieved by his reply. Apart from the ethical considerations of working with a less than thorough doctor, it had become important to her that Jonathan had a modicum of respect for the profession in which he was practising.

Suddenly he grinned at her and her heart gave a disconcerting lurch.

'How was your first day, then?'

'Not really what I'm used to,' Rose admitted. 'But interesting.'

She wasn't lying. But the most intriguing thing about the whole day was this man sitting beside her. She studied him surreptitiously from under her eyelashes. She had never met anyone like him before. How could she have? Her upbringing had been as different from his as it was possible to be. Her father and mother had worked hard just to keep their heads above water. Treats had been few and far between, but if material possessions had been in short supply, Rose had always felt treasured and loved.

She had always been studious, but she had never really been ambitious. After leaving school, without sitting A levels, she had done a secretarial course and had taken a job as a medical secretary with an out-of-town practice. It was there that she had realised that she wanted to do more with her life. The patients and their illnesses had fascinated her and she'd found herself becoming immersed in their lives. Soon the patients had been stopping by her desk on a regular basis to tell her the latest on their families, sharing their hopes and fears with her. One of the doctors had noticed how easily the patients spoke to her and how quickly she picked up the medical terminology and had suggested medicine or nursing as a possible career. She had taken her A levels at evening class and followed up her excellent results with four years studying for her nursing degree at Edinburgh University. The circle of friends she had formed there had shared her interests—walks, music, theatre and opera. University had introduced her to things she had never been exposed to before and she had lapped it up. After graduating, she had easily found a job she loved in Edinburgh, within walking distance of her flat.

It had been a warm, comfortable, if unexciting life. One she had cherished. Why, then, was she beginning to wonder if something had been missing?

CHAPTER THREE

'I'M HOME,' Rose called out, heaving a sigh of relief as she dropped her bags of shopping at the front door. The tube had been packed as usual, bodies pressed up against each other as the train had rattled and swayed. She had stopped off at the supermarket for something for tonight's dinner and had then had to complete the second half of her journey home. The walk from the station only took ten minutes but, laden as she was, combined with heels that, although sensible by most women's standards, were still an inch higher than Rose was used to, had felt every painful step of the walk home.

Her mother came out to greet her.

'How was it, love?' She reached for one of the shopping bags. 'Why don't you go in and see your dad while I put this away? Then you can tell us all about it over a nice cup of tea.'

'How is he, Mum? What sort of day has he had?'

'Not too bad. He ate his breakfast and his lunch, then we did the exercises the physio showed us. He's a bit tired now. I'll help him to bed once we've had supper.'

Rose found her father in his usual chair by the window. Her heart squeezed as she took in his useless arm and downturned mouth. The stroke had left one side of his body pretty much paralysed, as well as impairing his speech. Her father had been a vigorous man who had enjoyed going to football matches and playing cricket and golf, and now he was reduced to sitting by the window, watching the world go by. Rose knew how much he loathed needing help. If he would barely accept it from his wife, he hated taking it from his daughter. There had been a small improvement since he'd been discharged from hospital and Rose prayed with the proper treatment he'd continue to make progress.

'Hey, Daddy. How's it going? Seen any suspicious characters out there today?' She dropped a kiss on the top of his head and he gave her his lopsided smile.

'Hello, sweetheart,' he said. Although the words were indistinct, Rose knew that was what he was trying to say.

She sat down beside him and took his hand in hers. 'You have no idea what sort of day I've had, Dad.' She told him about the chocolates, Mr Chips, the visit to Jessamine's house, embellishing her stories to amuse him. Not that they needed much embellishment. She rubbed her stocking feet as she spoke, knowing she'd need a plaster or two before she could wear the shoes again.

'What's he like, then, this doctor you're working for?' Her mother appeared in the doorway, tea towel in hand. She had only very reluctantly agreed to Rose coming home to help look after her father. They had been so proud of her, the first in their family ever to get a university degree, and had wanted her to carry on building her career. In their minds, Rose knew they had her as Hospital Matron within a year or two. Rose had tried to tell them hospital matrons didn't exist any more, but they chose not to believe her.

Of course Rose had had to come home. She'd had to see her father for herself and she'd known the first weeks following her father's discharge would be tough, so she'd applied for, and been granted, five weeks' special leave. After that?

She shrugged inwardly. She'd have to see. Her mother wasn't getting any younger.

'Dr Cavendish?' Rose paused. How could she describe him? 'Well, he's young. Not much older than I am. About six foot and kind of lean. Apparently he's the son of a lord.'

'Well, I never. The son of a lord! What's he doing working as a doctor, then?'

'Apparently the practice belonged to his uncle who was doctor for the Queen's household. The uncle's retired now and Jonathan has taken over.'

'Is he poor, then? That he has to work for a living?' Rose's mother crossed over and plumped the cushions behind her husband's back. 'I know not all of the aristocracy is well off.'

'I don't think so, Mum. He drives a Lotus, although I suppose that could belong to the business. I don't really know much more about him. I can't say I've ever heard of his family.'

She closed her eyes and immediately an image of smiling green eyes and a mischievous grin flickered in front of her. How could she even begin to explain someone like Jonathan Cavendish to her parents when she could hardly explain her reaction to him to herself?

'Let's just say that I think the next few weeks are going to be interesting. Instead of acting as receptionist and medical secretary, it seems as if I'm to be nurse and chaperone.' Rose filled her parents in about Vicki before continuing, 'He has patients all over the country, and in Europe, and he's asked me if I can travel with him.' She looked at her mother. 'It does mean I won't be around to help as much as I'd like.' She paused. 'Maybe I should tell him I can't do it. Come to think of it, I must be crazy.'

Her father reached out and patted her on the arm. 'Do it,' he said. 'I want you to. It would make me feel better knowing that I'm not holding you back.'

Rose hugged her father, feeling his too-thin frame under her arms. Where had the strong muscular father of her teens disappeared to? He had always been there for her, now she wanted to be there for him and her mother. But he hated being dependent. And she had to make sure she didn't make him feel worse.

'By the way, Miss Fairweather phoned.' Rose's mother mentioned the name of the neurosurgeon Rose had seen after her father's stroke. 'She wants you to call her at the hospital. She wouldn't say any more. There's nothing wrong, is there, love?'

Rose felt a shiver of alarm but pushed it away. Her father's GP had recommended she see the specialist after discovering her father's stroke had been caused by an aneurysm. He'd told Rose that the condition often ran in families and to be on the safe side she should have herself checked out. Miss Fairweather had agreed and advised Rose to have an MRI. That had been on Friday and she had refused to let herself think about it over the weekend. She had been positive that there was nothing to worry about. After all, it wasn't as if she had any symptoms. No headaches, tingling sensations. Nothing. She dismissed the uneasy feeling that was creeping up her spine. No doubt the consultant just wanted to let her know that her results were all normal.

'I'm sure she just wants to let me know everything's okay, Mum. Don't worry. I'll give her a ring now.'

But when Miss Fairweather asked Rose to make an appointment to see her as soon as possible, Rose knew it wasn't okay. Had her results been fine, the neurosurgeon would have said so over the phone. Rose replaced the receiver, having made an appointment at the end of the week. She returned to the sitting room and her mother looked at her, alarm written all over her face.

'Not bad news, love?' she asked, the colour draining from her face.

There was no point in worrying her parents until she knew what Miss Fairweather had to say.

'No, Mum. Everything's fine,' Rose lied.

The following days at Jonathan's practice settled into a pattern. Patients would come to see Jonathan in the morning, then in the afternoon he would go out on visits, leaving Rose to type up notes if she wasn't needed. Some of the patients Rose recognised from the newspapers or TV, some she didn't recognise, but felt she should. Jonathan treated them all with the same easy grace and familiarity. Some afternoons she'd accompany him on his house visits, each home almost more spectacular than the last. Whenever Rose found herself thinking about her upcoming appointment with Miss Fairweather, she would push the thought away. There was no point in worrying until she knew what the neurosurgeon had to tell her.

But at home, in the privacy of her bedroom, she spent her evenings searching the net for information about aneurysms. None of it gave her much cause for optimism.

When Jonathan turned up for work in the morning, he'd sometimes look tired, as if he'd spent most of the night clubbing, although he never appeared hungover. And sure enough, there were photographs of him in the tabloid press, outside clubs and restaurants, with one glamorous woman after another on his arm. If it gave Rose a strangely uncomfortable feeling to see him with different women, she would dismiss the thought with a shake of her head. It was none of her business what he chose to do in his own time.

Once there was a photograph of him playing polo and she discovered that at least two of his free afternoons were given over to the sport. In the picture, he was swiping at an object with a long stick. Dressed in a white shirt and light-coloured trousers, his hair flopping over his eyes as he concentrated on his task, he looked like someone out of a regency romance. No wonder women seemed to find him irresistible.

She had managed to get in touch with Jenny, who had been delighted at the offer of some short-term work.

'I'm going mad having nothing to do,' Jenny had confided in Rose. 'I've sent out hundreds of applications but no luck yet. A bit of actual work experience can do me no harm. Especially if Dr Cavendish likes what I do and is prepared to put a word in for me.'

Rose had met Jenny the day she had gone to sign on with the agency. She was nineteen, having just finished her secretarial course, and full of boundless enthusiasm.

'Could you just tone down the hair?' Rose asked, remembering the spiky haircut. 'And perhaps remove the piercings, especially the ones from your nose and lip? Somehow I don't think it would be appropriate for the practice.' Even if quite a few of the patients had tattoos and piercings themselves.

'No problem,' Jenny said. 'I promise you you won't recognise me when you see me next.'

And true to her word, Jenny had turned up with hair neatly slicked into a bob, piercings removed and wearing a skirt that, while short, was just on the right side of decent.

She had regarded the consulting rooms with undisguised glee.

'This is a bit of all right,' she said. 'Now, where is this Honourable Dr Cavendish? And what do I call him? My Lord? Sir?'

Rose laughed. 'I think Dr Cavendish is just fine. Come on, I'll take you in to meet him.'

Happily, Jonathan seemed to take to Jenny. And the young girl, being smart and quick on the uptake, was soon ensconced behind the desk.

'He's a bit of all right,' Jenny confided. 'If he wasn't so old I could go for him myself.'

Rose laughed. 'He's hardly old. Twenty-seven.'

Jenny sent her a look that suggested that anyone over twenty-five was middle-aged in her opinion. Then she scrutinised Rose. 'But he's the right age for you.'

Rose smiled uncomfortably. 'I don't think I'm his type. Or he mine, for that matter,' she added quickly.

Jenny was still studying her critically. 'You know if you lost the glasses, maybe got some contacts, got a more modern hairstyle and some decent clothes, you'd be quite pretty.'

Rose couldn't make up her mind whether she was insulted or flattered. Get some new clothes and haircut indeed. Jenny watched too many films. Whatever, she knew Jenny didn't mean to be offensive.

'I appreciate your...' she searched for the right word '...opinion. But I'm happy the way I am. I like my clothes—they're comfortable. And I don't fancy poking my fingers into my eyes every morning and evening. Besides...' she glanced behind her just in case Jonathan was within earshot '...I'm not looking for a boy-friend. And if I were, Dr Cavendish wouldn't be him.'

'But...' Jenny started to protest.

'No buts.' Rose cut her off. 'Whatever thoughts are in that head of yours, get rid of them. I'm here to do a job. That's it.'

But after Jenny had returned to her work, she thought about what she had said. It was true she wasn't looking for a boyfriend, and even if she were, Jonathan wasn't for her, or she for him. Although he made her pulse race uncom-fortably, she doubted whether he took anything in life seriously. And even if he were her type or she his, she had far more important things on her mind than the dishy Jonathan Cavendish.

One morning, towards the end of the week, a well-known footballer came to the surgery, accompanied by his wife. Rose vaguely remembered reading about their wedding in a magazine she had picked up on the train. The footballer was even better looking in real life, his wife petite next to his six-foot frame. Whereas he was dressed simply in a pair of jeans and T-shirt, his wife was dolled up to the nines.

While Jenny organised drinks for them Jonathan called Rose into his consulting room.

'Mark and Colette came to see me a couple of weeks ago as they are thinking of starting a family,' he said. 'The last time they were here I arranged for them to have some tests. I have the results back. And I'm afraid it's not going to be the best news they ever heard. IVF is the only way forward for them unless they adopt. I'm going to arrange for them to have further investigations at the London Fertility Clinic, but in the meantime I think it would be helpful if you could sit in while I chat to them. If they agree.'

Rose nodded. She often sat in with the doctors in her surgery when they were giving unwelcome news. That way she could be there if the patients telephoned later, looking for clarification. A large number of patients were unable to take in everything they were told when they first heard that there was a problem.

The couple were happy to have Rose present. From their smiling faces, Rose knew they weren't expecting bad news. At least until something in Jonathan's face alerted Colette

'What is it, Jonathan? Something's wrong. I can tell from the way you're looking at me.' Colette's voice shook and Mark took her hand firmly in hers.

Jonathan pulled his seat around to the side of the table where Colette was sitting. His green eyes were full of sympathy.

'The initial bloods I took from Colette the last time she came to see me suggest that her ovaries are working normally. That's good. Although I think you should have the test repeated at the London Fertility Clinic. They will probably also suggest an ovarian scan, just to confirm the results of the blood test.'

'So there isn't a problem, then. We should just keep trying. We don't need to be referred.'

'There doesn't seem to be a problem with Colette.' Jonathan kept his voice steady. 'Although that's not a helpful way of looking at it. As if it's a problem belonging to one of the partners. Whenever couples are having difficulty conceiving, we like to think of it as a couple thing.'

'Come on, Jonathan. Stop beating around the bush. We come to you because we know we'll get straight answers.' Mark said.

'The difficulty is on your side, I'm afraid,' Jonathan said sympathetically. 'The semen sample you gave last week had very few motile sperm. The clinic will want to repeat the test again, but it would seem that you are unlikely to conceive without ICSI. That's an IVF procedure where Colette goes through IVF treatment to stimulate her production of eggs then her eggs are injected with one of your sperm. It's very successful. If…' He stressed the last word while looking Mark directly in the eye. 'If they can find sperm that's healthy enough to do the procedure.'

Mark looked as if he'd been poleaxed. 'Are you kidding? But I'm healthy. You won't find anyone fitter this side of London.'

'I'm sorry, Mark. As I say, you'll need to have more tests, but I'm pretty sure. That's why it's a good thing you came to see me sooner rather than later. The quality of your sperm is only likely to deteriorate the longer we wait.'

The shock on the couple's faces tore at Rose's heart. She could see Colette making a determined effort to pull herself together.

'I don't mind, darling,' Colette said. 'I don't care about having IVF as long as we can have a baby. Jonathan's not saying we can't have children and that's all that matters.'

But Mark was still looking dumbfounded. Suddenly he got to his feet and lurched out of the room. Jonathan looked at Rose, and reading the unspoken question in his eyes she nodded. 'I'll stay with Colette.'

Jonathan followed Mark, leaving the two women alone.

'Jonathan can't be right,' Colette said after a moment. 'It's not possible. Mark won't accept it.

We always assumed that if there was a problem it was me.'

Rose pulled a chair closer to where Colette sat and took her small hand. Her heart went out to the woman sitting next to her. In the last few days she too had had to face the real possibility that she might never have children. If she did have an aneurysm there would never be any children. Not even with IVF. A pregnancy would be too dangerous. Rose would never be able to carry a child. As her throat tightened, she pushed the thought away. She needed to focus on her patient.

'He'll come to terms with it in time, I'm sure. It's been a shock. And it sounds, from what Jonathan's being saying, that a child is not out of the question. It might just take a little help, that's all.'

'We didn't seriously think there was a problem, you know. We just came to see Jonathan because we wanted to make sure we were doing everything right for the baby from the moment it was conceived. You know, folic acid, vitamins. All that stuff. But when he heard we'd been trying for almost a year already, he suggested doing the tests—just to be on the safe side.'

'The procedure Jonathan's talking about isn't too awful, you know. And if you have a healthy baby at the end of it, what does it matter if you've needed a little help on the way?'

Colette still looked doubtful. 'We always assumed we were going to have a family. At least three. Maybe four.' She smiled wanly. 'I think he wanted to start his own five-a-side football team.' Her voice cracked. 'The thing is, I don't know if he'll agree to IVF at all. I think he might take it as a slight to his masculinity—you know how some men are. What will we do then?'

'You'll need to give him time, Colette. Once he understands exactly what's involved, I'm sure he'll come round.'

'You don't know that!' Colette protested hotly. 'You don't have any idea how we're feeling. To think one day that you have everything happiness, wealth, fame, only to have your dreams stripped away the next.'

A wall of pain slammed into Rose.

Colette had no idea that she understood only too well.

* * *

Eventually Jonathan and Mark returned. 'We just walked around Regent's Park for a bit,' Jonathan told Colette. 'Mark's had time to think it over, and he's agreed that the best thing to do is have you both seen at the fertility clinic. You just tell me when it suits you and I'll fix up an appointment. Then I'll see you back here and we can take it from there. Okay?'

The couple just nodded. Rose knew it would take them a little time to get their heads around what Jonathan told them and her heart went out to them. As Colette had said, what did wealth and fame matter if you couldn't have what your heart truly desired?

Jonathan was unusually sombre after the couple had left.

'They'll be okay, won't they?' Rose asked.

He pulled a hand through his thick, dark hair. 'I hope so. They've had a shock. They're a lovely couple. Despite Mark's fame, and despite his reputation for being a little wild on and off the field, he's down-to-earth, kind. So is she. If ever a couple would make great parents, it would be them. And as I told them, ICSI has a very high success rate. Even higher than getting pregnant naturally. As long as the embryologists can find any motile sperm.'

Jonathan gave his head a little shake as if to banish whatever thoughts were troubling him. He picked up tickets Mark had left on the desk when he'd first arrived.

'You fancy going to a football match?' he asked. 'Mark left some tickets for the Arsenal game next Saturday. I would go, but I already have tickets for the one-day International at Lords. I like football, but next to cricket…' He grinned. 'No competition, I'm afraid.'

'No, thanks,' she said regretfully, thinking of her father. 'Although you have no idea how much I'd like to accept. My Dad and I used to go all the time before I left home. He hates missing all the matches. He's been an Arsenal fan all his life.'

'Then give the tickets to him,' Jonathan said, thrusting them in her direction. 'They're for a box. He'll get a grand view.'

Rose wished she could accept on behalf of her father. It would be just the tonic he needed to lift his spirits. But getting him up and down flights of steps was more than she and her mother could manage.

'I wish he could go,' she said softly.

'So take him,' Jonathan persisted.

Rose turned away so Jonathan wouldn't see the tears that sprang to her eyes. 'He had a stroke about two weeks ago. He lost the use of his left side. He doesn't go out much any more. He hates the indignity of being seen out in public, and even if he didn't, until I get a new car that can take his wheelchair, he's pretty much trapped at home.'

Jonathan took a long look at her. Then he grinned and his eyes glittered. Rose's stomach flipped. 'You probably don't know this, but my family motto is *Where there's a will there's a way*. Actually, it's not, it's something far grander, but it means the same thing.'

Before Rose could ask him what he meant, his next patient arrived and Jonathan led him into his room.

'I'm so sorry,' Miss Fairweather told Rose. 'I really wish I was giving you better news.'

The room swayed as a wave of nausea hit Rose. She had known that there was a good chance the news would be bad, but she hadn't allowed herself to believe it. Now her worst fears were being realised. She did have an aneurysm.

Gathering her courage, she sat up straight in the hard backed chair and looked the young consultant in the eye.

'Okay, so what are my options?'

'You have two choices. You do nothing, and decide to live with the aneurysm.'

'Which would mean what exactly? Please, Doctor, don't mince your words. I need to know exactly what I'm facing.'

Miss Fairweather leaned forward. 'It is possible that you could live the rest of your life without the aneurysm bursting, but if it does, and there is no way of predicting how likely that would be, you could have a stroke and depending on the severity, you could be left with a number of physical problems—loss of speech, the use of your legs, or…'

'Or I could drop down dead,' Rose finished for her. 'Suddenly and without warning. Mmm, doesn't sound like much of a choice to me. What are my other options?'

'You can have an operation to remove it. Unfortunately there are a number of risks associated with the procedure too.'

'Such as?' Rose gripped her hands together to stop them shaking. Her mind flicked to her parents. They'd be devastated. She was their only child and knowing her father he would blame himself for passing on the genetic condition to his much-loved daughter. The same thing that had caused his stroke. How long had he been living with the time bomb inside his head? How long had she? She pushed the thoughts of her parents away. There would be time enough later to think about them. Once she had all the facts. Once she knew what she was going to do.

'Death, stroke. The complications of surgery aren't too different from the results should your aneurysm burst, I'm afraid. The problem is where your aneurysm is. The location makes the surgery riskier than usual.'

'Not a great choice, then.' Rose smiled wryly at the consultant. She *had* asked for her to be straight with her.

'On the other hand, if we manage to remove it through surgery, there is a good chance you could live to a ripe old age, have children, do everything you hoped for before this.'

'And if I don't? What then?' Rose knew the answer, but she wanted to hear it from Miss

Fairweather. Maybe she had misunderstood what she had read about the condition on the internet.

'I'm sorry. You wouldn't be able to risk having children. It would put too great a strain on the blood vessels inside your brain. Otherwise, the risks are as I outlined earlier. But you don't have to decide straight away. You should go away and discuss it with your parents and boy-friend. Have a think. Make sure you understand the risks of both options. However, I wouldn't leave it too long. If you do decide to have the operation, the sooner you have it the better.'

Ten minutes later, Rose was outside the hos-pital. Although summer was supposed to be on its way, the wind still had a wintry feel to it. Wrapping her coat tightly around her, Rose stumbled to a bench and finally let the tears that had been clogging her throat for the last half an hour fall. She could die. Maybe tomor-row, maybe in ten years, maybe twenty. Miss Fairweather admitted that there was no way of telling. How could she live the rest of her life not knowing if every minute was going to be her last? On the other hand, if she had the op-eration Miss Fairweather had suggested, she could still die. Or be left paralysed, in a wheel-chair—or worse. That prospect didn't have much going for it either. In fact, the thought was even worse than death. At least that would come quickly. The thought of a slow death, having to be looked after by her elderly parents, was infinitely worse. Being dependent on anyone didn't bear thinking about.

She blew her nose loudly. Behind her she could hear the sound of a baby crying. She had never imagined that she might not be able to have children one day. Never hold a child in her arms. Maybe never again go for a walk in the rain, watch an evening sky change colour as night approached. Never learn how to ski, or speak Spanish. All the things she had told herself she had plenty of time for. Perhaps it was just as well that she had never met anyone she cared enough about to marry. What should she tell her parents? Nothing. Not yet. They had enough on their plates right now with Dad's stroke without having to worry about her.

So there would be no more tears. No self-pity. She would do as Miss Fairweather had suggested. She would think long and hard about what to do. In the meantime she'd treat every minute of her life as if it were her last. No more hiding away. No more not doing something because it was too expensive, or scary, or any of the hundred reasons she had given herself in the past. From now on, she would say yes to every experience life had to offer. From now on, she would make the most of every second she had left.

During the long nights that followed her appointment with Miss Fairweather, Rose tossed and turned, trying to decide what to do. In the end, she decided she couldn't have the operation. What if it went wrong? And she ended up like her father, or worse? How would her mother cope with two invalids? Besides, if her father hadn't had a stroke, she would never have known about the ticking time bomb inside her head. She would have carried on living her life the way she was doing now.

In the small dark lonely hours of the night, she had tried to draw up a list of things she wanted to do before...well, before it was too late, but had given up on the list when she'd come to number fifty and scored it through. Instead, she promised herself she would try and live each day as best she could, taking any opportunities that came her way. She still couldn't get her head around the fact she could die any time. She felt so healthy and life had never seemed so painfully precious and filled with promise.

CHAPTER FOUR

JONATHAN habitually asked her if she wanted to go to lunch with him, but she always refused. The first sunny lunchtime, she asked him if it would be okay if she took a little longer than her usual half-hour.

'I'd like to take my lunch to the park,' she said. 'It's such a beautiful day and I could really do with some exercise. Jenny will be fine on her own for an hour.'

'Good idea,' he said. 'I'll come with you. There's a deli on the way, I could pick up something to eat from there. It will make a change from the stodge they serve up in my club. God, it reminds me of school dinners.'

Rose was taken aback, but she could hardly refuse. 'You can share mine, if you like. My mother always insists on making my lunch and she puts enough in to feed an army. I think she worries I don't eat enough.' Rose laughed. 'I eat like a horse, I just don't seem to put on any weight.'

Jonathan's eyes slid over her and she felt her cheeks flush under his gaze. She pulled her cardigan around her. What on earth had possessed her to say that? And as far as offering to share her lunch, she had the distinct impression Jonathan wasn't used to having egg and cress sandwiches or whatever her mother had packed for her. Didn't people like him have caviar or some other such stuff for snacks?

'Come on, then, if you're sure you've enough. We'll pick up a couple of coffees on the way.'

As they walked Rose felt inexplicably tongue-tied. It was different when they were working. Somehow, without patients to discuss, it was different.

After picking up their coffees they found a bench looking over a small lake. The good weather had brought out mothers and children, or was it their nannies? There were also a number of people strolling or jogging. Rose handed Jonathan a sandwich and lifted her face to the sun.

'Have you lived in London long?' he asked between mouthfuls.

'I was brought up here. My parents have lived in the same house all my life. I went away to university. Edinburgh, actually. I have an aunt who lives there so I was able to stay with her. It helped keep the cost down. What about you?'

'I boarded at Gordonstoun. I was almost six when my father sent me there. I studied medicine at Cambridge.'

Rose had heard of Gordonstoun. She knew it was a famous and very expensive school in the north of Scotland where many of the rich sent their children. She had also heard that the regime was very tough.

'Isn't that where Prince Charles went?'

'Yes. But long before my time.'

'How awful to be sent away to school when you were so young. Weren't you terribly homesick?'

Jonathan turned to her, looking surprised. He really did have the most amazing eyes, Rose thought. Dark green, and ringed with an even darker shade. He had the kind of eyes that made her feel he could see right into her soul.

'You know, I never really thought about it. It was just something that happened. I suppose the first few years were hard. I missed my home.

But all the other boys were in the same situation. And there were the holidays—at least, some of the holidays. My father was away a lot, so I stayed with schoolfriends most of the time.' His eyes darkened and he looked away into the distance as if he found the memory unpleasant.

'I don't think I could ever send my child away. Especially at that age,' Rose said thoughtfully. 'But I guess your parents must have had their reasons. Would you send your child?'

Jonathan's eyes narrowed. If it were possible, he looked even bleaker. Rose could have kicked herself. She had no right to question the way he had been brought up.

'My child? You know, I can't say I've ever thought about it. Children have never really figured in my plans for the future. Somehow I don't ever see myself having them. They require commitment. And I'm not that kind of guy.' He grinned. 'Life is too full of possibilities to settle on one.'

Rose eyed him speculatively. Maybe when he met the right woman he would feel differently. Then again, maybe not. Somehow she couldn't see Jonathan giving up the lifestyle he enjoyed for the restrictions a domestic life would inevitably bring.

'I don't think my mother would have sent me if it had been up to her. She died when I was five, and my father sent me away soon after the funeral,' he continued after a moment.

Rose was shocked. How could a father send away a child who had just lost his mother? And not just down the road, but several hundred miles. An image of Jonathan as a little boy wearing long shorts and a peaked cap, standing alone outside the school while his father drove away, flashed through her mind and her heart twisted with sympathy for the little boy he'd been. What kind of man was his father if he could do that to his son? Rose thought if she ever met him, she would dislike him intensely. No wonder Jonathan seemed to have little faith in the joy children could bring. It was ironic: Jonathan didn't want children, although he almost certainly could have them; and she wanted them, desperately, yet couldn't have them. If she had been able to have children, she would never send them away. She would have kept them close to her, making the most of every precious moment with them. A wave of sadness washed over her. She forced her thoughts away. Thinking like that was pointless.

'I'm so sorry, Jonathan. I can't imagine what it was like for you. To lose your mother when you were so young and then be sent to boarding school.'

'Don't we all do things because we have to? I know duty is considered an old-fashioned concept, but you must believe in it too. You came back here to look after your father. You must have had a life in Edinburgh.'

Rose forced a smile. 'Of course. But as you say, sometimes we have to do what is right rather than what we want. My parents needed me.' She shrugged. 'So I came. My life in Edinburgh can wait.' *If* she had a life to live.

'No boyfriend?'

'No one serious.' She wanted to change the subject. It was far better for her to keep her mind off her future—and the possibility she might not have one.

'Why did you decide on medicine?' she asked him, genuinely interested. From what she had gathered, Jonathan's family was rich enough for there to be no need for him to work at all.

Jonathan smiled ruefully. 'As I told you, my

uncle was a doctor. He was apothecary to the Queen. He used to talk to me all the time about cases he had came across when he was still working in a hospital. I loved listening to him and I can hardly remember a time when I didn't want to be a doctor. I needed to do *something* with my life. My father hoped I'd take over the family business, but it wasn't for me.'

'But Harley Street.' Try as she would, Rose couldn't quite keep the disapproval from her voice.

'My uncle built up the practice. People liked coming to see the man who looks after the Queen's health. You can't get a better recommendation than that. I was going to set up a practice somewhere else, but then he became ill and wasn't able to carry on. Back to duty, I guess.' He took a gulp of his coffee. 'I couldn't let him down.'

'You don't miss real medicine, then?'

He looked at her, amusement making his eyes glint.

'You know, even the rich and famous get ill. In the end, birth and wealth don't prevent you from experiencing health problems. Like Mark, for example.'

Yes, she should know how arbitrary illness could be. Despite the warmth of the sun, she shivered.

He looked at his watch. 'Speaking of which, I have to visit Lord Hilton this afternoon. You remember his wife coming in to see me on your first day? She has arthritis and he has terminal cancer. He really should be in hospital, but he refuses point blank. Says he has no intention of dying anywhere except the home he's lived in all his life.' Jonathan studied Rose thoughtfully. 'How would you feel about coming too? If I remember correctly, she took a shine to you.'

'Poor Lady Hilton. I had no idea. Yes, of course I'll come. If you need me.'

What Rose didn't know and what Jonathan neglected to tell her was that Lord and Lady Hilton lived a hundred miles from London and that they were sending their private helicopter to bring Jonathan to their country home. The helipad was a ten-minute drive from the surgery.

Rose had never been in a helicopter before, let alone one that had leather seats as wide as armchairs in the back.

'You didn't tell me we were flying to our

visit,' she accused Jonathan when he pulled up at the helipad on the Thames.

His eyebrows quirked in the way she was beginning to know well. 'You didn't ask. About fifty per cent of my patients live outside London. In fact, they sometimes fly me out to see them when they're on holiday. Wherever that might be.'

'They don't see someone locally? Surely that would be better?'

Jonathan gave her a half-smile. 'I see you have a lot to learn, Rose Taylor. Most of my patients are so rich that is doesn't occur to them not to fly their doctor out. In the same way that they'd fly out their hairdresser or stylist. They like to see the same physician.' He shrugged. 'And I don't mind going. I've known some of my patients most of my life.'

It was a different world. One where Rose didn't know the rules. But it was a job. As long as she got paid and as long as Jonathan's patients didn't suffer, who was she to judge? And, she had to admit, it was exciting to be part of it, even for a short time. She sucked in a breath as she remembered the promise she had made to herself. *Live every day to the full.* At least

working with Jonathan was bringing new ex-
periences and every minute was exciting. How
much of the excitement was down to new ex-
periences and how much was due to being in
the company of the man sitting next to her, she
didn't want to think about.

Jonathan gave her a radio set to wear, partly to
drown out the noise of the engine and partly so
they could hear each other speak. Below her the
river Thames cut its way through London. She
could see Buckingham Palace and the Tower of
London as well as the pods of the London Eye
revolving slowly.

'Have you been in it yet?' Jonathan asked,
pointing to London's newest tourist attraction.
'Sorry, silly question. Of course you have.'

'As a matter of fact, no. I haven't had the time.
I'd love to some time.' One more thing to add
to her steadily growing list. 'Have you?'

'Once or twice.' He grinned. 'One of my
friends is having a party there in a few weeks'
time. You should come.' It was another invitation, but Rose knew that Jonathan was just
issuing them out of politeness. If she accepted,
he'd probably be dismayed.

Soon they were leaving London behind and

passing over the countryside. A short time later they flew over a house bigger than most hotels Rose had stayed in and were touching down in what was the back garden, but which anywhere else would have been a park.

'Oh, my word,' Rose said as she stepped out of the helicopter. 'The last time I saw a house like this it was in a film. How many people live here?'

'Just Lord and Lady Hilton. His sons live in London. They come up when they can.'

A man dressed in the traditional garb of a butler walked towards them. Rose smiled. It was just like being on a movie set.

'Good afternoon, sir, miss,' the butler said. 'Lord and Lady Hilton are expecting you.' He turned to Rose. 'What name should I say?'

'This is Miss Taylor, Goodall. She's a nurse at the practice. Lady Hilton and Miss Taylor have already met.'

'Lord Hilton is in his bedroom. Lady Hilton said she'd like a word before you go in to see him, if that's all right?' Goodall said.

Jonathan chatted to the butler as they walked the few hundred yards to the front door. From the snippets of conversation Rose caught, it seemed they knew each other well. Following behind, Rose took in the formal garden with its neatly trimmed hedges and flower beds. Dotted throughout were nude sculptures, some modern, some more classic. It must have taken an army of gardeners, Rose reckoned, to keep it looking so perfect.

Inside, the hall was twice as large as the one in the town house belonging to Jessamine. There was a grand central staircase in the middle of a polished marble floor. Someone had lit a fire in the huge fireplace that dominated one side of the hall and with the large bowls of brightly coloured flowers it had a cheerful air. Despite the grandeur, Rose knew immediately she was in someone's much-loved home.

Goodall showed them into a room which, while as grand as the hall, had been decorated in thoughtful, homely fashion. Large squashy couches with brightly coloured cushions and a rug that had seen better days added a splash of colour to the otherwise muted room. Light was flooding in from the floor-to-ceiling windows overlooking the front garden, but a fire burned brightly in this room too. After the coolness outside, it was almost suffocating.

Mr Chips jumped down from an armchair and pattered across to them, his tail wagging. Rose bent to pat him, and in return received ecstatic doggy kisses on her hand. In an armchair next to the window was Sophia Hilton. Her silver hair was perfectly coiffed but despite the heat in the room her face was pale. Rose was sure there were more lines around her eyes and mouth than there had been when they'd first met. She was dressed in thick stockings and a tweed skirt and the hand she held out to Jonathan had the slightest tremble. Rose knew immediately that this was a woman who was under enormous strain, but desperately trying not to show it.

Jonathan bent down and kissed the older woman on each cheek.

'Sophia, how are you? And Lord Hilton?'

'Jonathan, dear boy. How good of you to come and see us. And Miss Taylor, an unexpected pleasure to see you again too. Jonathan told me you're filling in for Vicki until she's well enough to return.' Her mouth trembled slightly. 'Giles isn't good, I'm afraid.'

Jonathan pulled up a chair next to Lady Hilton and Rose sat on the sofa opposite. 'Tell me what's been happening,' he said gently.

'He's fading. He hardly eats at all now. He says he has no appetite. He gets up for an hour or two but that's all he can manage.' She dropped her voice to a whisper. 'We're losing him, I'm afraid.'

'You're both still sure you don't want to try another bout of chemotherapy? I could have him in hospital by this afternoon.'

Lady Hilton shook her head regretfully. 'He won't hear of it, I'm afraid, and I have told him I'll respect his wishes. That's why I don't want you to try and persuade him. He's too weak to put up a fight, so he made me promise to speak to you before you saw him.'

'The chemotherapy might help.'

'Will it prolong his life?'

Jonathan looked her directly in the eye. 'I'm not going to lie to you. It might give him a little more time, ease his symptoms, but, no, the outcome will be the same.'

'And the chemotherapy will make him feel even worse in the short term, won't it?'

'He didn't react to it very well before. So, yes, I'm guessing he'll feel even more rotten than he does right now.'

'Then nothing's changed since we last had this conversation. Except it's getting closer.'

'Have you thought any more about bringing in nurses to help? I thought Rose here might be able to convince you. She worked in general practice before she joined us in London.'

Rose leaned forward. 'If it's okay with you, I'd like to see your husband and have a chat with him before I advise you. But Dr Cavendish is right, there are lots of options that would allow you to keep him at home but help you keep him comfortable at the same time.'

'Of course.' Lady Hilton stood. 'I'll take you both upstairs.'

Rose and Jonathan found their patient sitting in a chair by the window with a rug over his knee. A book lay by his side, and a still full cup of tea sat ignored on the table next to him. His eyes were closed and his face had the grey gauntness that Rose had seen too often before. She knew immediately that Lord Hilton didn't have much longer.

His wife touched him gently on the shoulder.

'Darling, it's Jonathan and his nurse come to see how you are.'

Eyes flickered open and as they focused on

his wife, a look of such love that Rose had rarely seen filled the pale blue eyes. Her heart contracted.

'Jonathan, my dear boy. How are you? And your family?' The voice was weak but clear.

'Father is always asking after you.' As he spoke, Jonathan placed his fingers on the old man's wrist.

'Any word of getting married yet? Isn't it time?'

Jonathan laughed. 'No. Can't find a woman who is crazy enough to have me.'

'What about this girl here?' For a moment Rose squirmed. He couldn't be alluding to her as a possible wife? The poor man must be confused.

'This girl, as you put it, is my nurse. Victoria's pregnant. Unfortunately she's being very sick again so has to take time off. Rose is filling in for the time being.'

Rose stepped closer so that she could be seen. 'Dr Cavendish thought I might be able to help make you more comfortable—or at least suggest some things that could help.'

Rose watched carefully as Jonathan finished his examination. While he was doing that she was assessing how Lord Hilton moved and how much pain he seemed to be in.

'Why don't we have a little chat while Jonathan talks to your husband?' Rose said to Lady Hilton. 'You can tell me what help you have at the moment.'

Once they were back in the sitting room, Rose broached the subject of nursing care.

'I don't want strangers looking after him,' Lady Hilton protested.

'What about a night nurse at least?' Rose suggested gently. 'Someone to sit with him through the night so you can get a good sleep?'

'There's Goodall,' Lady Hilton said firmly. 'He'll attend to Giles if he needs anything at night. He also helps him shave and wash. He's been with him for thirty years and knows his ways.'

Rose had to admit that having someone to help who Lord Hilton knew well would be far less stressful than bringing in new faces at this stage.

'I know Dr Cavendish—Jonathan—is likely to suggest a morphine pump. That way the pain can be controlled. Will you consider it? You'll need to have a nurse call at least every second day to check on it, but that shouldn't be too intrusive.'

Lady Hilton blinked furiously. 'Why did Victoria have to be unwell now of all times? Oh, don't mind me, I'm just being selfish. Of course, it's important that she looks after herself now that she's pregnant. But Giles knows her. He would have been happy to have Goodall fetch her from town every day.'

'I'm sure there will be equally good nurses locally that would be happy to come to the house.'

'That would mean interviewing people. It would be terribly time-consuming. I don't want anything to interfere with the time we have left. I know there's not much time.' Her eyes locked onto Rose's and she could see the spark of hope there. But just as quickly it was replaced with resignation. 'You don't have to pretend otherwise, my dear. I know it and Giles knows it.' She paused for a moment. 'Couldn't you come? He's met you and he seems to have taken to you. And Jonathan wouldn't have brought you here if he didn't think highly of you. We could arrange for you to be collected and brought back every day. Please say you'll agree.'

Although Rose felt for the older woman's distress, she knew what she was suggesting would be impossible. Just as she was trying to find the words to let her down, Jonathan walked back into the room.

'He's sleeping now. Goodall and I helped him back into bed. I think he should have something more regular for the pain, however. I can come and see him whenever you want, but analgesia as and when he wants it would be better.'

'Miss Taylor was just suggesting the very same thing. But she tells me a nurse will have to come in regularly to check the pump. I asked her whether she could come. What do you think, Johnny? Could she?'

Jonathan looked at Rose. 'I'm afraid I need her in London,' he said.

The old lady looked so woebegone that Rose couldn't help herself. With Jenny manning the desk, she could come and help the Hiltons. It would keep her busy. She had too much time to brood as it was.

'What about if I came after my shift? Would that work?'

Jonathan frowned. 'Would you excuse us for

just a moment?' he said, and taking Rose by the elbow steered her out of earshot.

'I know you want to help, but don't you have your own situation to think about? It'll be too much.' For a second Rose thought that somehow he had found out about her condition, even though she knew it was impossible. 'Coming here and putting in a full day's work before going home to help out with your father. I've your health to think about too. The last thing I need or want, is to have to find another nurse.'

'It's not as if I'm run off my feet at the surgery.' Rose glanced across at Lady Hilton who was studiously looking out the window. 'I just wanted to help. Anyway, there's at least three free afternoons a week where you don't have any patients. I know you keep them free for emergencies or unscheduled home visits, but so far they've been quiet and I've just been twiddling my thumbs. I could come here then.'

Jonathan's eyes followed hers. Despite the determined look and the upright posture, Lady Hilton needed help and they both knew it.

'I'll agree to it on one condition,' Jonathan said. 'You come here only on those free afternoons and on the other two we shuffle my schedule around so that there aren't patients booked in for when you're here. Jenny and I can cover the odd drop in or emergency between us. If that suits you, we have a deal.' He didn't need to say what they were both thinking. It was unlikely that the arrangement would be required beyond a few weeks at the most.

He smiled sadly at Rose and her heart skipped a beat. 'Thank you for offering. I've known Lord and Lady Hilton all my life. Anything that will make these last few weeks and days easier for them would mean a great deal to them…and to me.'

Jonathan told Lady Hilton what they had agreed, emphasising that they still needed to get Jonathan's schedule sorted out but that he didn't think it would be a problem. The relief in her eyes brought a lump to Rose's throat.

Jonathan turned down Lady Hilton's invitation to dinner. 'Next time, I promise. But it's getting late, and I really have to get Rose home. I'll phone you tomorrow morning and let you know what we've managed to sort out between us.'

The journey back in the helicopter was a more

subdued affair. Rose found herself wondering about Jonathan. On the one hand, he seemed to like nothing better than to be partying along with his social set; on the other, as a doctor, he seemed to genuinely care about his patients. She had been guilty of making assumptions about him that appeared to be no more than figments of her imagination. In that regard she was no better than the press. She slid a glance in his direction. Why couldn't she have met someone like him before? Before her world had been turned upside down? And why did she have the sinking sensation that what she was feeling was a good deal more than she should for her boss?

CHAPTER FIVE

ON SATURDAY morning, she was sitting reading to her father when there was a knock at the door. Rose glanced out of the window, surprised to see a large four-by-four parked outside. Baffled, she answered the door to find Jonathan standing there with a broad smile on his face. He was dressed in faded jeans and a short-sleeved shirt. It was the first time she had seen him in anything apart from his suit and if anything he looked even more handsome. Certainly more approachable.

For once the sun was shining and although it was cool, there was a hint of summer in the air.

Open-mouthed, Rose stood back and let Jonathan in.

'Who is it, love?' Her mother came to stand behind her.

'It's Dr Cavendish, Mum.'

'Please call me Jonathan,' he said, holding

out his hand and smiling charmingly at her mother.

'Why are you here?' Rose asked, suddenly conscious of the small house with its comfortable but worn furnishings. Then, aware of how rude she sounded, she apologised. 'I'm sorry, I'm just a little surprised to see you. I didn't think you even knew where I lived.'

Jonathan's smile grew wider. 'Your address was on your file.' Then he frowned. 'I should have phoned, but I thought we had an arrangement?' In the cramped dimensions of the hall she could smell his aftershave.

'Arrangement?' Rose echoed.

'The tickets to the match. Remember? I promised I'd find a way to get your father there. If he'd still like to go, that is.'

Rose was bewildered. 'You've come to take my father? Don't you have a cricket match to go to?'

'There will be other matches,' he said dismissively, but Rose knew enough about cricket to know that despite his words he was giving up one of the most looked-forward-to events of the year. 'I'm planning to go to a party afterwards. Perhaps you'll come too?'

Rose shook her head, still confused. He had given up his day to do something for her father, a man he'd never met, and he wanted her to go to a party. Her heart skipped a beat. 'I couldn't. I've nothing remotely suitable to wear. Besides, I'm needed here.' It wasn't the whole truth. Her father was improving daily and required only minimal help now. But her at one of Jonathan's parties? Not on your life. What on earth would she have to say to his friends or them to her? The idea was ridiculous. Nevertheless, she had to admit to a small stab of regret. It had been ages since she'd been out. Besides, she had to admit that she was intensely curious about what sort of party it would be. Like everything else these days, it would be another new experience to add to her growing list.

Suddenly aware that they were still standing in the small hall, Rose remembered her manners.

'You'd better come in.'

She ushered him into the small sitting room. Her parents looked up, curious.

'Dad. This is Dr Cavendish. He's come to ask if you'd like to go to the football match this afternoon.'

Jonathan crossed the room and shook her father's hand warmly. 'I'm pleased to meet you, Mr Taylor. Your daughter tells me you're an Arsenal fan. Well, it so happens that I have tickets to the match today and I wondered if you'd like to come?'

'That's kind of you, son,' Rose's father said. His words were still slurred and Rose doubted that Jonathan would be able to understand what he was saying. 'But my leg's a problem. I don't think I could get up the stairs.' Although he was continuing to improve, pretty much managing to get himself washed and dressed, he had to lean heavily on a stick to walk. Rose doubted he'd be able to manage more than a few metres without a wheelchair.

'I have a plan for that,' Jonathan said. It seemed as if Rose had been wrong and that he could make out the words her father was trying to say. 'If I told you that I thought Rose and I can manage to get you there and to your seat without too much trouble, what would you say?'

Rose saw her father's eyes light up and her heart ached for him. She remembered how he had taken her to football matches when she'd been young, hoisting her onto his shoulders so that she could see better. They had never missed a home match until she'd left for university in Scotland.

'I don't know, lad. Maybe you should take my Rose and go on your own. You'd enjoy it better.'

'I'm not going to the match, Dad. Unless you go too. And I don't think Dr Cavendish plans on staying. He has something else on.'

'Did I say that?' Jonathan asked innocently. 'Can't imagine why. There's nothing I'd rather be doing, but I don't care to go on my own. So you and Rose would be doing me a favour by coming with me.'

'Go on, love,' Rose's mother prompted. 'You haven't been out of the house since…' She paused and Rose guessed she still found it difficult to admit even to herself. 'The stroke. A bit of fresh air will do you the world of good. And I could be doing with getting your father from under my feet for a few hours.'

Rose knew her mother didn't mean a word of it. Her parents still loved each other deeply. Her mother wanted to bring some joy back to her husband's life. Rose also knew her father wouldn't go without her.

'In that case, I say yes, I'd love to go.'

With Jonathan helping, it was difficult but manageable to get her father along with his wheelchair into the roomy back seat of the car Jonathan had brought instead of his sports car. When they arrived at the football stadium, Jonathan flashed something at the security guard and drove up to the front gate. With him on one side of her father and her on the other, they used the lift to reach the box where they were to be seated.

'Always wanted to see the footie from one of these fancy boxes,' Tommy said when they had seated him with a rug over his lap. 'Never could afford it.'

'We can go inside the lounge and have lunch first, if you like?' Jonathan suggested.

Tommy shook his head. 'You two go. I'm just as happy to stay here now I'm settled.'

'And I'd rather stay with you, Dad.' Rose turned to Jonathan. 'But please don't let us keep you from your lunch. We'll be fine here until the match starts.'

'Then I'll go and fetch us something to have here. I don't want to eat on my own. Any preferences?'

Several minutes later, Jonathan returned with a tray full of various goodies to eat. Rose noticed that he'd included several items that would be easy for her father to eat with his one good hand. Once more she was surprised and touched by his thoughtfulness. Her father was a proud man and wouldn't have touched anything that meant Rose had to help him in public.

As they waited for the match to begin, Jonathan and her father chatted about previous matches. It was the first time she had seen her father looked so animated since his stroke and she sent silent thanks to Jonathan. Doing this had surely been outside expected behaviour for an employer. She guessed it was to repay her for seeing to Lord Hilton. Whatever the reason, Rose knew she was in danger of falling for her boss. Her heart gave a sickening thud. Two more things she'd have to add to her list. Watching a football match from a box and falling in love for the first time.

* * *

Despite her father's team losing in the final seconds of the match, it was a good day and Rose was disappointed when it came to an end.

Jonathan drove them home, dissecting the game in excruciating detail with her father while Rose sat back in her seat, allowing their chat to wash over her. She was falling for a man with whom she had nothing in common. Why now? When, even if he could ever feel the same about her, she had no future to offer him? Perhaps it was because she didn't know what the future held that she believed herself in love? If what she was feeling *was* love. It was certainly lust. Infatuation. Every time he smiled her stomach somersaulted. Whenever he was in the room her heart would start pounding and she would feel short of breath. If he touched her, even the slightest pressure of his hands as he passed her a mug of coffee or a set of notes, her knees would go all rubbery. But it was more than that, she knew, and her heart dropped to her boots. Regardless of his reputation as a womaniser, he was kind and gentle. Would anyone else have given up what he had just to take the ailing father of an employee to a football match? Rose doubted it.

Her mother was waiting for them when they arrived home. She too seemed better for having an afternoon off, although Rose knew that the sight of her father looking as he once had was worth more to her mother than any number of afternoons with her feet up.

Jonathan helped her father settle back into his chair. Rose could hardly look him in the eye in case he read her mind. It would be too mortifying for words if he guessed how she felt.

'I've asked Rose if she'd like to come to a party with me tonight,' Jonathan said suddenly. 'But she's turned me down.' He turned the full voltage of his charm on her mother, who was already putty in his hands.

'Rose?' Her mother turned to her. 'You didn't say no, did you?'

'I can't go, Mum. I'm needed here,' Rose said.

'Don't be silly. We can manage. Besides, you could do with some fun. You've been looking awfully peaky lately.' Rose could see the worry in her mother's searching look.

'And I don't like my staff to look peaky,' Jonathan added. 'I promise you, if you get there and you aren't enjoying yourself, I'll bring you straight home. Or we can miss the party. Do something else.'

Rose capitulated. The truth was, right now she could think of nothing she wanted more than to have more time with Jonathan. Who knew how many opportunities she had left? If she only had a short time left, this was how she wanted to spend it.

'Okay, you're on,' she said. 'On one condition. Tonight you come with me and meet some of my friends.' She held her breath as she waited for his reply. Whatever he wanted from her, she had to know if it included wanting to spend time with her on her own territory. If he wasn't simply using her as an excuse to avoid whatever demons he had in his life, she needed to know that too.

'You're on.' Jonathan grinned. 'Lead me to it.'

Jonathan sat in the pub feeling, he had to admit, slightly awkward. Rose had been engulfed by a load of her friends and he hadn't seen her for at least ten minutes. Someone, he couldn't remember who, had stuck a pint of beer in his hand and instructed him to drink up. Why was

he here? And more importantly, why was he
so driven to find out more about Rose Taylor?
There were any amount of women he could be
dating, ninety nine per cent of them less prickly
than her and none of whom would be insisting
that he get up and sing. He groaned internally.
Apparently getting up on stage was part of the
evening entertainment. And Rose had made
no attempt to hide her glee when she had told
him that he'd be expected to stand up and do
his bit. Still, he was damned if he was going to
admit defeat. He just prayed that none of the
paparazzi had followed him here. Thankfully,
it was extremely unlikely. It would never cross
their minds that he'd be found in a pub on the
outskirts of London.

The pub was packed for a special Scottish
themed night, with people coming from all over
London for it. The place was filled with laughter and the chinking of glasses.

Rose squeezed her way into the seat behind
him. Instead of the usual tied-back hair she had
loosened it until it fell about her shoulders in
a sleek glossy wave. Her eyes sparkled and a
small smile played on her lips. He had never
seen her so animated.

Suddenly there was a call for silence and after a few minutes everyone quietened down. A man Rose had introduced earlier as Jack, an old friend, had climbed onto the make-shift stage and was speaking into a microphone.

"Most of you know Rose,' he said.

There was loud applause as everyone cheered and stamped their feet. Rose blanched slightly and muttered something under her breath. 'What some of you don't know is that Rose composes her own songs and plays the guitar as if she's making love to it.'

There were more wild cheers. Jonathan slid a glance at Rose. She played the guitar. This was the first he had heard of it. And wrote her own songs.

'I know she'll be happy to play us a tune—if we give her a loud cheer.'

There was more applause and stamping of feet. If anything, the uproar was even louder than before. Rose was shaking her head, her hair falling across her crimson-stained face. Then she got to her feet and amid more cheering made her way to the stage.

She took the microphone from Jack's hand. 'Sorry, everyone,' she said into the mike. 'I didn't bring my guitar with me tonight. So I'm afraid I can't play for you.' There was a sigh of disappointment then Jack turned round, holding a guitar which someone had passed to him.

'Sorry, darling,' he said. 'But we just so happen to have one here for you to play. Go on, you can't let everyone down.'

Reluctantly, Rose took the guitar from him. Someone pulled a chair across for her and she sat down, trying a few tentative chords. All the noise dropped away until there was complete silence.

'Okay, I'll play one song for you.' She held up a finger to emphasise her words. 'I'm going to play "*Fear A Bhata*". It's a Gaelic song my mother used to sing to me when I was a little girl. She sang it to me whenever she was missing Scotland, which was often. I'm playing it tonight for everyone who is far from home.'

In the silence Rose strummed a few chords then her husky voice wrapped itself around the packed room. Jonathan didn't need to be able to understand the words to know it was full of longing and loss. The sound of her voice did something to his heartstrings that he'd never experienced before. He was transported to a

ANNE FRASER   133

world where people longed for something they couldn't have. The Rose up there on the stage was a revelation to him. In the place of the shy, mousy Rose he had come to admire and respect was a beautiful woman who sang as if she knew all about heartache and loss. A woman with depths to her he had never guessed existed. A woman he found exciting yet restful. In that moment he knew that he was falling for Rose and the thought scared him witless.

When the final notes of Rose's song had faded away, there was complete silence followed by a burst of applause. There were cries of 'More' but Rose just shook her head and passed the guitar back before stepping off the makeshift stage.

Jonathan was finding it difficult to concentrate. For once he didn't know what to do. She slid back into the seat next to him, her cheeks flushed and her eyes bright.

'You didn't tell me you could sing like that!' Jonathan said.

Rose smiled briefly. 'It's not as if it's ever come up. It's just something I do for fun. When I'm in on my own and it's raining outside.

Sometimes, when something touches me, I make up my own songs. I guess it's my way of relaxing.' She glanced at him and he could see the teasing look in her eyes. 'I've never sung in public before. I didn't think I could.' If he had found her interesting before, now he knew he wanted to know everything about this woman who was so unlike anyone he had ever met.

Then there was a sudden movement as chairs and tables were lifted and piled up at the sides. A group of three had taken to the stage. One was carrying an accordion, the other two fiddles.

Rose flashed him a grin. 'Can you dance?' she asked. 'It looks like you're getting away with singing tonight.'

Jonathan breathed a sigh of relief. 'Depends what kind of dancing you're talking about. I do a fairly mean waltz and not a bad foxtrot, but I'm getting the distinct impression that it's not the kind of dancing you're talking about, is it?'

'Nope.' Rose's grin grew wider. 'They do two types of dancing here. One is Scottish country dancing, the other line dancing. You must have learned Scottish country dance at your school in Scotland, surely?' Jonathan felt a wave of relief. They had been taught the formal Scottish dances with their intricate steps. He could do that all right. But, still, there was that suspicious little smile hovering on Rose's lips. It unnerved him.

He stood up and as the band struck up a tune and invited everyone to take their places for an eight-some reel, he held out his hand to Rose. 'Shall we?' he asked.

But if he'd thought he was going to be dancing a dance that he had learned, he soon found out he was badly mistaken. Oh, the steps were the same, but the pace was quite different. It all happened at breakneck speed and in response to the fervour of the dancers, the band increased their tempo. Soon he was part of a dervish dance where everyone's feet were moving at the speed of light. As he whirled Rose around, her hair fanned out behind her. Then he was dancing with another partner who was forcing him to move ever faster. Not before time, the dance ended and Jonathan was able to get his breath back. But the respite was brief. Immediately the music struck up again. The Canadian barn dance was followed by the Boston two-step and the Highland Scottische. All carried out at breakneck speed. He just gave in to it and soon he found he was enjoying the exhilarating pace and being swept up by the rest of the dancers. For the last dance, the tempo slowed and the band asked everyone to take their partners for a St Bernard's waltz.

He pulled Rose into his arms, breathing in the scent of her as she placed her head on his shoulder. At first she was stiff in his arms, but as the music continued he felt her relax against him. It was strange how they seemed to fit together.

'So what do you think so far?' She raised her face and looked into his face with her amazing china-blue eyes. 'Not your cup of tea, I'm guessing?'

'Then it's clear you don't know me at all, Rose Taylor. How about we go to that party Jessamine mentioned for our next date?'

His words took even him by surprise. Just what was he getting into here? He felt her pull away, but he wrapped her back in his arms.

'Our next date?' she said, her face flushing. 'But this isn't a date, is it? Just two friends out together.'

'Is that what you really think?' he said. 'Come on, Rose, pretending doesn't suit you. You and

I both know that there's more to it than that. I want to get to know the real Rose Taylor and I suspect you're not immune to me either.'

She raised her face to look him directly in the eye. 'We both know that we can't have a relationship,' she said flatly.

'Why not?' he asked.

She looked back at him. 'You know why not,' she said steadily.

'I'm not sure I do.'

'I don't think mixing work and personal life is a good idea.'

'Why? Aren't we doing that now? I'm having a good time. Aren't you?'

'Yes but…' She trailed off, seemingly at a loss for words.

She was thinking she wasn't from his world and he wasn't from hers, Jonathan mused. Admittedly, they had different upbringings, different friends, different lives, but what the hell did it matter? Not to him. It did to her, though. Her expressive face couldn't hide her obvious disapproval of him and the frivolous lifestyle she believed he led. She seemed so sure they had nothing in common. But he had never felt this at ease in a woman's company. And he knew he had never wanted a woman the way he wanted her right now.

'Can't we just go out and have fun? As friends?' he asked, knowing damn well that he had no intention of just staying friends with her. 'Let's just see where this takes us? No promises on either side. Just two people who enjoy each other's company getting to know each other better.'

'I'm not very good at casual relationships, Jonathan,' she said. 'I know it's not very modern, but there you go, that's the way I am. I can do nothing about my background, but I won't change who I am just to suit you.'

'I'm not asking you to. I won't push you to sleep with me if that's what's worrying you.' He was unable to stop himself smiling at the thought of Rose naked in his arms. 'I promise I'll be a perfect gentleman. I'm guessing you could use a friend right now.'

'I do have friends,' Rose protested, waving her hand in the general direction of the room.

'But we can never have too many, can we? Come on, what do you say? Have a little fun. If you don't need friends, you do need something to take your mind off work.' He dropped his voice. 'And what's happening at home.'

If only he knew that what was happening at home wasn't the whole of it. And hadn't she told herself she would make the most of whatever time she had left? Take tonight, for example. Although Jack had tried to get her to sing in public before, she had always refused; the thought had scared her senseless. But then she had remembered her promise to herself and had forced herself to take the guitar. By closing her eyes she had been able to let herself pretend she was back in her room, alone, and once she had started singing she had lost herself in it. She had poured her heartache, the loss of her future into the music. And it had felt good. The applause had taken her by surprise; she had almost forgotten there were other people in the room.

When she'd opened her eyes, it had been to meet Jonathan's green eyes looking at her with what? Admiration? Surprise? Something was changing inside her, and she wasn't convinced it was just down to her illness. Somehow being with Jonathan made her feel as if she could do anything. The thought took her breath away. This wasn't supposed to happen. This wasn't part of her plan. But if she couldn't offer him a future, well, neither was he suggesting one. She held out her hand. He looked at her in surprise before enveloping it in his. His hand was cool in hers, his long fingers those of a surgeon. A thrill ran up her spine. More than anything else in the world, she wanted to know what it would feel like to be held in his arms. To have his mouth pressing down on hers. To lose herself in him—even if it was only for a short time.

'Okay.' She found herself smiling. 'I give in. I'll go with you to the party tomorrow.' She wagged a playful finger at him. 'But only because I've never been to a party on a yacht before.'

Jonathan grinned. 'If that's what it takes, I've plenty more types of parties to tempt you with.'

CHAPTER SIX

IT WAS bucketing down, Rose saw as she peered out from her bedroom window the next morning. So much for the start of summer. Her stomach was a mass of butterflies as she thought about the day to come. If she hadn't been so determined to follow through on the promise she had made to herself she would have been tempted to find an excuse not to go. Once again, she wondered if she was admitting the whole truth to herself. It wasn't just her vow to grab life with both hands while she could, it was that the life, just tantalisingly out of her reach, now held Jonathan. Who knew how long he'd be in her life? And she wanted to spend every minute she could with him. She was making memories that would have to last her a lifetime, however long that might be.

Pushing away the morbid thoughts, she considered her meagre wardrobe critically. The trouble was she didn't have the vaguest idea what one was supposed to wear to a party on a yacht. In the end she settled on her standby little black dress she always wore when she needed something more formal than her usual skirts and jeans. The best thing about it was that it was cut in a way that made her bony frame look sophisticatedly curvaceous instead of the sharp angles she was used to seeing.

By the time she had showered and dressed, the rain had stopped and the sun was shining. Maybe the day wouldn't be a complete washout after all.

Jonathan arrived to collect her, looking as sexy as hell in his faded jeans and short-sleeved shirt. He whistled in appreciation when he saw her and Rose was uncomfortably aware of the blush warming her cheeks. With a bit of luck he wouldn't notice.

The first surprise was that the yacht wasn't on the Thames. Jonathan had laughed when he'd noticed her bewilderment.

'I don't think many people keep their boats on the Thames. No, this one is moored off the coast of the Isle of Wight. They're sending the helicopter for us.'

Is that how everyone travelled in his circle?

Rose thought a little grumpily. What was wrong with a car, although, come to think of it, getting to the Isle of Wight by road was, of course, impossible. Her head was beginning to ache. It had been a crazy idea to come. She was sure to be completely out of her depth.

Jonathan slid a glance in her direction. His face took on an uncharacteristically sombre expression.

'You're not having second thoughts, are you?' he asked.

It was on the tip of Rose's tongue to say, yes, she was and would he mind just dropping her off at the nearest station? But she bit the words back. She promised herself that she was going to try and be more adventurous and she was damned if she was going to bail out just because she was terrified she wouldn't fit in. After all, what was the worst that could happen? If everyone ignored her, she could...what? Swim back to London?

'I'll look after you, I promise,' Jonathan said. 'They're really a good bunch of people. Some a bit wilder than others, but nothing too outrageous.'

Giving in to the inevitable, Rose made herself

relax. At least, with Jonathan promising to stay close by, she wouldn't be left on her own.

The yacht was unlike anything Rose had ever seen before. For a start it was enormous, almost the length of a football pitch, and all gleaming white lines and stainless steel.

There were a number of people already there. Half of the guests were in bikinis or swimming costumes, the other half were dressed informally in shorts or jeans. Rose felt overdressed and uncomfortable. But there was no way, no way at all, she'd wear a swimming costume to a party, especially this early in the year.

Someone handed them a drink as soon as they stepped on board. Taking a sip, Rose grimaced and, looking around in case anyone was watching her, tipped her drink over the side of the boat. It was far too early to be drinking champagne.

Seconds later, to her dismay, Jonathan was swept up in a crowd and carried away. So much for his promise to watch out for her. To be fair, he wasn't to know just how cripplingly shy and out of her depth she felt right now. Rose leaned against the side of the boat, wondering how long she would have to stay before making her excuses. She knew she should introduce herself to one of the chatting groups, but she just couldn't make her hands let go of the rail.

'Hello.' A soft deep voice broke into her reverie. 'And who are you?'

Rose whirled around to find a blond-haired man with slightly unfocused eyes looking at her. Clearly he had been at the champagne.

'I'm Rose Taylor. Jonathan's nurse,' she said politely, proffering a hand.

'Pleased to meet you, Rose Taylor, Jonathan's nurse. I'm Henry. It's my sister's party.'

Rose craned her neck wondering which one of the guests was Henry's sister. It could have been any of the elegant women clustered on the deck. She could just make out the top of Jonathan's head in the centre of a group of attentive females. As if sensing her eyes on him, he turned and caught her eye and raised a questioning eyebrow. She shook her head slightly. Now someone was talking to her, she was no longer sticking out like a sore thumb.

Henry reached over and lifted Rose's glasses from her face. Her unease mounted as everything around her blurred. She reached for her glasses but Henry grinned and hid them behind his back. 'Hey, you're not bad looking when a person can see your face.' He swayed towards her, breathing the smell of stale alcohol on her face. 'Trust Jonathan to keep you as his little secret.'

Embarrassed and repulsed, Rose stepped back. But Henry stepped closer until she was almost pinned against the side of the boat. Over Henry's shoulder, she looked for Jonathan but all she could see were blurry shapes.

'Please give me my glasses back,' she said as steadily as she could. The last thing she wanted was to cause a scene in front of all these strangers.

Henry waved them in front of her. 'A little kiss in exchange?' he slurred.

Rose snatched the glasses from his hand. At least now she could see properly. Over Henry's shoulder, she caught Jonathan staring at them, frowning. Something in her face must have told him that she was extremely uncomfortable. Within moments he was by her side.

'Hey, Henry. Can I have my guest back?' Jonathan said smoothly. 'I think I should show her around.' He took Rose by the elbow and steered her away.

'Henry is best avoided, I'm afraid. He eats girls like you for breakfast.'

Suddenly furious Rose shook his arm off.

'And what makes you think I can't handle him? Just because I don't mix with the rich and famous every day of my life, it doesn't mean I don't know how to handle snakes like him. If he hadn't taken my glasses and I couldn't see, I wouldn't have needed you to…rescue me.' She almost spat the last words, her mortification at being the centre of attention causing her to direct her fury at Jonathan. She should never have come, no matter what promises she had made herself. Being mortified wasn't on her list of must dos!

Jonathan laughed. Immediately the anger drained from her.

'I should have known better. Of course you could handle Henry. One look from those diamond eyes is enough to cut anyone down to size.'

The world stood still. Jonathan reached over and gently lifted the glasses from her face. 'You do have amazing eyes, you know.'

Rose felt the strength go from her legs. He shouldn't be looking at her like that. It wasn't fair. He was making her feel as if she was just as beautiful as the rest of the women, and that was rubbish. Next to them, she was like a gawky schoolgirl. She snatched her glasses back from his hands. Thankfully everything swam back into focus. Why, oh, why did he have to smile like that?

Desperate for him not to see her blushing, she turned on her heel, almost falling over in the process. Once again, he reached out and grabbed her, steadying her against him. She could feel the heat of his body, smell his aftershave and it was doing all sorts of confusing things to her head. She looked up to find amused eyes looking into hers. Did he know the effect he was having on her? Of course he did. Someone like him would be used to it. She pushed against his chest and drew herself up to her full height. 'You were going to show me around?' she said stiffly, wishing desperately that she could think of something more amusing, more light-hearted to say.

The grin still very much in evidence, Jonathan

indicated a flight of steps leading down into the boat with a nod of his head.

'Let's start inside.'

At the bottom of the steps was a sitting area filled with people, laughing and chatting. Jonathan steered her through the group, stopping only to say a brief hello and promising to come back later for a proper chat. But before they could get to the other side of the room, a girl with hair like a silver waterfall ran up to Jonathan and threw her arms around him.

'Darling, I've being looking for you everywhere.' Rose was conscious of curious eyes on her. But she was damned if she was going to let anyone else see how uncomfortable she was. She left Jonathan and wandered off by herself.

Off the main sitting area there were a number of bedrooms which, although small, were kitted out with the latest electronic equipment. Flat-screen TVs and state-of-the-art speakers. Each bedroom had a small but fully equipped bathroom.

She threaded her way back through the main sitting area. Jonathan had disappeared, so she went back up the stairs. The deck wrapped around the boat, and there was a jacuzzi at one end, what was it called? The prow? Several guests were in the jacuzzi, lapping up the sun. A couple of waiters and waitresses circled around, carrying trays of drinks and canapés. Rose helped herself to an orange juice and a tiny tart of something unrecognisable but delicious. Thankfully Henry was nowhere to be seen.

'Here you are,' Jonathan said, appearing at her elbow with the blonde. 'I've been looking all over for you. May I introduce Summer? Summer, this is Rose.'

Well, of course she'd be called Summer with hair like that. The blonde smiled at her, but there was a speculative look in her eyes that made Rose wonder.

'My goodness,' she said. 'Where did you buy your dress? Was it from some vintage market?'

Ouch. Was everyone at this damn party determined to make her feel small? In the past she might have mumbled something and walked away, but that had been before... Before she'd known there were more important things in life to worry about than rude, obnoxious people who had nothing better to do than make themselves feel superior at her expense.

'Yes, it was. How clever of you to know that,' Rose responded. 'I love wearing clothes that other people have loved wearing in the past. It makes me feel as if I know them a little.'

She took in Summer's outfit. The blonde was wearing tights that looked as if they'd been fashioned from the skin of a tiger and a gold lamé dress that just covered her bottom. Although she did look gorgeous, it wasn't the kind of outfit Rose could ever see herself wearing in a hundred years. It was far too trendy and far too short for a start. No, whatever they thought of her clothes, she preferred the simple black dress she was wearing. And if it was a few years out of date, she didn't give a hoot. In fact, she had just about as much as she could take of being given the once over and found wanting. She should have stuck with her original gut instinct and stayed well away. What would she and this crowd ever have in common?

But just as she was searching for the words to make her excuses, a dark-haired girl with an impish expression sidled up to Jonathan and tucked her arm in his.

'I've been admiring your dress ever since you arrived,' she said. 'I'm sure it's exactly like the one I saw last week on the catwalk in Milan. And I have to say, it looks better on you than it did on the model. Don't you think so, Summer?' The new arrival flashed Summer a look from green eyes.

'Rose, could I introduce Lady Ashley, my cousin? Ashley, this is Rose.'

Ashley held out a slim hand and grasped Rose's in a firm grip. 'I'm so very pleased to meet you. Johnny's being telling me all about you. Are you enjoying yourself?' She turned to Summer and said sweetly, 'Summer, I don't suppose you would mind very much grabbing one of the waiters? I'm famished.'

Summer glared at her before stalking off. Ashley winked at Rose. 'She's harmless really. She just has the hots for my dear cousin here. She can't resist having a go at the opposition.'

Opposition? Her? Was she out of her mind?

Out of the corner of her eye, Rose caught a glimpse of Jonathan elbowing his cousin in the ribs.

'And my dear cousin likes to exaggerate,' he

drawled. 'I'm sure Summer has no interest in me whatsoever.'

Ashley raised one perfectly groomed eyebrow. 'Don't be naïve, sweetie. You know her type as well as I do. Just because her daddy earns millions, she thinks she should be marrying into aristocracy. And I'm afraid it's you she has her sights on.'

'I'm sure Rose isn't interested in whatever fantasies are filling your brain, Ash.' Although his voice was cool it was evident in the way he looked at his cousin that he held her in very real affection. 'Besides, I've made it perfectly clear that I'm not in the market for a wife. Not now. Maybe never.'

'Hey.' Ashley laid a hand on his arm. 'You mustn't talk like that. Just because Uncle Charles can't stay married for five minutes, it doesn't mean some people don't make a go of it.'

'I think that's enough on that subject for now.' Jonathan's tone was light, but there was a note of warning in his voice. 'So, Rose, have you seen enough? What do you say we get out of here?'

There was nothing that Rose wanted more.

But she didn't want to drag Jonathan away from the party. Especially when they'd only been there for an hour.

Suddenly there was a cry of alarm from the other side of the boat. 'David! Help me, someone! Oh, God, I can't see him.'

Jonathan spun away, making for the other side of the boat where a crowd was forming. Rose followed close behind. Everyone was looking down at the water, muttering and pointing.

'David jumped in. I can't see him.' The girl's voice was frantic. 'I told him he'd had too much to drink to even think of going in the water, but he wouldn't listen. God, where is he?'

Jonathan was pulling off his shoes and top.

'Where did he go in?'

The distraught girl pointed. 'He dived in over the side. I think he hit his head. Please, Johnny, help him.'

Jonathan balanced himself on the side of the railings before diving into the water. Everyone waited in silence as he surfaced and looked around wildly. Then he dived again and again, each time coming up and shaking his head. Finally, just as some of the other men were preparing to join him in the water, he rose to the surface again. This time he was holding a body in his arms. Rose held her breath as willing hands hauled them back onto the deck. The man Jonathan had pulled from the sea didn't seem to be breathing. There were cries of distress and alarm. The girl who had called out dropped to her knees and cradled the head of the man in her lap.

'David,' she cried. 'Please wake up. You have to wake up.'

Rose pushed her gently aside. 'Let me have a look,' she said quietly. By this time a sopping-wet Jonathan had joined her on deck. She bent her head and breathed into the unconscious man's mouth. One twice, fifteen times. She watched to see if his chest would move, but it didn't. She looked up to find Jonathan's eyes on hers. She knew he was thinking the same thing she was. They would have to get the water out of his lungs before they could get him breathing again.

Together, they worked to pump the water from his lungs until, to their relief, David coughed, bringing up a large amount of water.

'Has someone called for an ambulance?' Jonathan asked.

'I have,' Ashley replied.

'Okay, I need a hand to get him into the little boat,' Jonathan said. 'Tell the ambulance to meet us at the jetty.'

David had regained consciousness, but looked confused and bewildered. His head was bleeding copiously. Jonathan examined the wound with gentle fingers. 'It's pretty superficial,' he said. 'Does anyone have anything we could use to stop the bleeding?'

Rose ripped a piece of fabric from her dress and used the material to staunch the wound. Oh, well, as Summer had pointed out, it *had* seen better days.

'What happened?' David moaned.

'You idiot,' his girlfriend cried out, before bending over and hugging him. 'You could have killed yourself. If it hadn't been for Jonathan and his friend, you'd be dead. Don't you ever do that to me again.'

Rose touched her on the shoulder. 'David's going to be fine, but we still need to get him to hospital. Inhaling sea water isn't the best thing for a person's lungs. Is there a medical kit on board? I'd like to put a proper bandage on his head.'

A medical kit appeared in Jonathan's hand. He quickly found a bandage and wrapped it around the piece of cloth from Rose's dress. It was crude, but it would do until the ambulance arrived.

Rose led David's distraught girlfriend to the side, while Jonathan and some of the other men lifted the small boat onto the deck and laid him inside. Then Jonathan looked at her, so she moved forward and stepped into the boat.

'As soon as we get this lowered, I'll join you,' Jonathan said.

Rose nodded and hiking her skirt up settled herself in the boat beside the injured man. In the distance she could hear the wailing of an ambulance.

As soon as the dingy was back in the water, Jonathan let himself down the ladder and joined her. He started the outboard motor and headed the boat back towards land. Rose kept a close eye on David's vital signs, but it seemed as if he was going to be okay. Jonathan was still drenched to the skin but showed no sign of discomfort.

When they reached the shore, the ambulance crew took over. They asked a couple of questions and Jonathan brought them up to date. Soon the ambulance was speeding away with David on board.

'Well, that's one way of ending a party,' Jonathan said grimly, watching the ambulance disappear. 'I guess he's going to have a sore head in the morning. I don't suppose you want to go back?'

'Not on your life,' Rose said vehemently. Then she could have bitten her tongue. She softened her voice. 'Look, it was kind of you to ask me to the party, but all this…' she waved her hand in the general direction of the yacht '…is not really my cup of tea. I'm sure your friends are great but, well, to be honest with you, I think I'd rather be out for a walk and then curl up with a good book. I know it all sounds very boring, but it's what I like.' She smiled. 'An added bonus is that I don't spend too much of my time rescuing my friends after they've jumped into the water under the influence and bashed their heads.'

'Okay, then. Look, no one is expecting you back home for another few hours so why don't we spend the rest of the day together and you can give me another chance? We can do whatever you want to do.'

'Slum it, you mean?'

Jonathan looked offended. 'I wouldn't consider it slumming. For some crazy reason, Rose Taylor, everything you do interests me. I'd also like to show you my other side.' He grinned and Rose's heart flipped. She couldn't believe he was really interested in her. She so wasn't his type and that was okay, it wasn't as if there could ever be anything between them, even if she didn't have this awful thing in her head. And even if he was the most exciting, gorgeous man she had ever met. Anyway, when he realised she truly wasn't kidding about her life, she wouldn't see him for dust. The thought sent her heart crashing to her boots. However awful the day had been so far, she wasn't ready for it to come to an end.

'When do you have to be back?' he asked.

'I'm not expected back until later tonight. One of Mum's friends is coming around for a visit later, and she's offered to help Mum get Dad into bed.'

'I could do with a change of clothes. How would you like to see my country house?' Jonathan grinned at her.

Rose pulled a face. 'Of course you have two houses. Why didn't I think of that?'

'Er, two houses here, plus the family home. I'm afraid there are another couple abroad.' He held up his hands. 'Nothing to do with me. My father collects houses like other people collect hats.'

'What? And just passes them on to you?'

Jonathan looked offended again. 'He gave me the town house. I admit that. Simply to avoid inheritance tax. But the one I'm planning to take you to is all mine. I think you'll find it interesting. Come on, what do you say? In fact, I'd really like your opinion. Ashley tells me I should decorate, but that's not really my forte and I haven't a clue what to do.'

'Why don't you pay an interior designer to do it? Their taste is bound to be much more like yours.' But she couldn't help feeling curious. What kind of house did Jonathan like to call home?

'Okay, then,' she capitulated. 'Why not? But I'm warning you, I'll tell you truly what I think—no messing around. I have to be honest, your town house is not my cup of tea.' She had seen it once when she had brought over some urgent letters for Jonathan to sign. The opulent interior hadn't seemed to fit with the Jonathan she was getting to know.

Jonathan's grin grew wider. 'To tell you the truth, it's not mine either. That's what happened when I let an interior designer loose—that was my cousin's idea—not mine by the way. It's like living in a boutique. Or a hotel. I'm not going to risk that again.'

So a medical secretary, a nurse, now an interior designer. If she wasn't careful, she'd be taking on the role of housekeeper too.

Once they had flown back to London the drive took just under an hour. Jonathan drove fast, but he was a careful driver and Rose settled back and watched the countryside flash past. She still wasn't sure what she was doing or, more to the point, what Jonathan wanted from her.

Eventually he turned into a long sweeping driveway. Instead of following the driveway, Jonathan pulled up outside a small house close to the gates. It was a typical gatehouse of the type Rose had seen at the gates of every stately home she had ever visited—as a fee-paying visitor, that was.

'Here we are,' Jonathan said as he switched off

the ignition. 'We can go up to the main house and say hello to Mary later. She's the cook.' His eyes softened. 'Actually, she's a damn sight more than a cook. She's lived in the house since before my mother died. She's been like a second mother to me.'

He opened the door to the gatehouse and stood aside for Rose to enter. There was a small hallway, not much bigger than the one in her parents' house. To the left was a sitting room. It was furnished simply with deep leather sofas and a couple of side tables. There was an open fireplace and in front of it a worn but beautiful rug. All along the side were bookshelves, and directly opposite where they were standing a window seat overlooked the garden. On the walls were more paintings like the ones in Jonathan's consulting rooms. The house was unexpected and a delight. Rose instantly fell in love with the room.

'There's another sitting room through here and a dining room and a kitchen. Upstairs there are three bedrooms.'

Whatever Rose had expected, it wasn't this. Somehow she'd imagined something full of boys' toys, not this cosy little house. It seemed she was constantly getting Jonathan wrong.

'It's perfect,' she said. 'I can't see why you want to redecorate.'

Jonathan looked baffled. 'That's what I keep telling people. But Ashley seems to think it needs to be brought up to date.'

'I wouldn't change a thing,' Rose said adamantly. 'But, of course, it's not my house.'

Jonathan smiled at her and her heart did the strange little somersault it always did whenever he looked at her that way.

'In that case, I'm going to leave it the way it is. I like it. I can put my feet up on the table and I can turn around without worrying I'm going to knock over some ornament or another.' He paused for a moment. 'It feels more like home than any place I've ever lived.'

While Jonathan disappeared to get changed, Rose walked across to the bookshelf. There were the usual classics as well as a number of thrillers. There was also a pile of medical journals on the floor. On the side table was a photograph of a woman and a man. They had their arms wrapped around each other as they picnicked on the lawn. Rose recognised the gatehouse in the background. She picked up the photograph for a better look. The woman was rather plain looking, except for her eyes which were an arresting shade of green. The man could have been a younger Jonathan.

'Your parents?' she asked Jonathan when he returned.

He took the photograph from her and Rose caught her breath at the look of sadness that washed over his face.

'Yes,' he said heavily. 'It was taken on their seventh wedding anniversary. Mother died shortly after that.' He placed the frame back on the table. It was the only photograph in the room. 'It didn't take long for Dad to remarry. Six months, I think it was. He recently divorced his third wife. I guess he's a man who can't stand his own company.'

The bitterness in his voice shook Rose.

'Don't you get on with him?'

Jonathan laughed harshly and turned away from her to look out of the window.

'No. I guess you could say we don't get on. He didn't want me to go in for medicine. He thought as the only son I should take over the family business. I don't think he's ever forgiven me for not doing what he wanted. And I can't forgive him for forgetting about my mother so soon. He could at least have waited a decent period before marrying again.'

'Maybe he wanted to provide some stability for you? Perhaps he thought he was doing the right thing?' She walked across the room and touched him on the shoulder. 'Perhaps he's never been able to forget her and that's why he keeps marrying?'

Jonathan turned to face her. He ran a finger down her jaw. 'Ah, Rose. Trying to find the best in people all the time. When will you learn that there's not many people like you?'

'Hey, don't make me out to be some kind of saint. It makes me sound so boring.'

'One thing you're not is boring, Rose Taylor.' She held her breath as he tipped her face so he could see into her eyes. She was sure he was going to kiss her and her heart was pounding so hard she could almost hear the rush of blood in her ears. She closed her eyes, anticipating the feel of his lips on hers.

His mouth brushed hers in the lightest of kisses. She opened her eyes to find him looking down at her intently.

'Come on, let's take a walk up to the main house. We can see if there's any dinner going. If not, we'll go back to the village to find a pub. How does that sound?'

What just happened there? Rose thought, bewildered. Had she misread all his signals? It was perfectly possible. Once again she was reminded that she didn't know how men like Jonathan operated. All she did know was that she felt a thudding disappointment.

Jonathan read the confusion in Rose's eyes. She wasn't to know it had taken all his willpower to pull back from her. For the first time ever with a woman he wanted to take it slowly. She was becoming too important for him to rush things. He wanted to woo her gently—take his time, make everything perfect. She was too important to him to treat her as if she were simply another woman he took to his bed. He was beginning to suspect that he had found the missing part to him and the thought filled him with dismay. In his soul, he knew Rose wasn't someone who would love lightly. He owed it to her, and to himself, to be sure he wouldn't hurt her before he let things go any further. He bit back a groan.

He had never thought about a future with any woman before, but it seemed finally he might have met the woman who could change his life. He was in deep trouble.

It was a substantial walk up to the house. As they turned a bend in the driveway the house came into view and Rose gasped. It was a beautiful large Georgian house, the facade grand but graceful. There were too many windows to count but Rose guessed that there had to be at least ten, possibly more, bedrooms.

'It's beautiful,' she whispered. 'Quite stunning.'

'I suppose it is,' Jonathan said thoughtfully. 'But to me it's just the house I was brought up in.'

They walked up a number of steps towards an ornate front door and stepped into the hall.

'Anyone at home?' Jonathan called out. 'It's Jonathan.'

His call was greeted with silence. 'Mrs Hammond, the housekeeper, is probably in her office. Let's have a look in the kitchen. Mary, our cook, is always in there. She's probably grabbing a snooze. Dad wanted to retire her years ago, but she won't have it. Says she'll go mad without anything to do. You'll like her. She still bakes every afternoon.' He sniffed the air appreciatively. 'In fact, I'm sure I can smell scones.'

He led her across the hall and down some stairs and along another passage with several doors leading off. 'In my grandparents' day this was the servants' quarters. At that time there were at least twenty people working in the house. Now it's just Mrs Hammond and Mary who live in. A couple of women come from the village every day to help with the cleaning. Most of the rooms are shut up. Dad only keeps the rooms he's using open, unless he has visitors. Then we draft in some more help.'

They followed the smell of baking to the end of the passage and turned left into the largest kitchen Rose had ever seen. There was an enormous old-fashioned range to one side and a huge scrubbed pine table in the centre. On top of the table was a pile of recently baked scones as well as a carrot cake. On the other side was a bowl of chopped vegetables. In the corner of the room was an armchair with a figure that, as he'd anticipated, was sleeping, snoring gently.

Jonathan tiptoed towards the sleeping figure and gently touched her on the arm. The old woman mumbled in her sleep before coming to. Faded grey eyes looked up in confusion, before the woman's face broke into a wide smile.

'Master Jonathan! How many times have I told you not to sneak up on me like that? You'll frighten me to death one of these days. I keep telling you, this old heart can't take surprises.'

'And I keep telling you that there's nothing wrong with your old heart,' Jonathan teased.

'Who is this?' Mary struggled to get up. Jonathan placed a helping hand under her elbow until the older woman had heaved herself to her feet.

'This is Rose. A friend.'

The faded grey eyes grew sharp. 'A friend, huh? You've never brought a friend down here before. Does she know what she's letting herself in for? And what does Lord Cavendish have to say?'

'Who I'm friends with has nothing to do with my father, Mary.'

Rose stretched her hand out. 'I'm pleased to meet you, Mary. I don't think Lord Cavendish and I are very likely to meet. Jonathan and I aren't that kind of friends.' All the same, she couldn't help feel offended. Cheek.

'Hey, don't mind me, love.' She ruffled Jonathan's hair as if he were about ten years old. 'Jonathan here could do with a good woman. Someone with a bit of heart instead of the type he usually runs around with.' She sniffed disapprovingly.

'Shall I put the kettle on?' Rose offered, not knowing what else to say.

'No, away you go and wait in the drawing room. I'll bring up a tray shortly.'

'I'd rather stay down here, if we won't get in your way,' Rose said. 'It's such a cosy room.'

Mary sent another sharp look Rose's way. Then she seemed to make up her mind. Her mouth turned up in the faintest of smiles.

'I think you might have found a good 'un, Master Jonathan. None of those other women would think of stepping down here to say hello to an old woman. It would be beneath them.' Her eyes grew moist. 'Not like your mother, love. No airs and graces about her. She was never happier than when she was down here, sitting in that chair, chatting away to me, her dress and her hands covered in paint. She'd even roll up her sleeves and tackle a bit of baking when the mood took her. She just laughed when your dad told her it wasn't appropriate.' There was another loud sniff. 'This place has never been the same since she passed away. Bless her soul.' Now Rose knew who had painted the wonderful landscapes that hung on his walls at the surgery and his home. Jonathan's mother had been a wonderfully talented artist.

She sat back down in her chair while Rose put the kettle on the stove and found the tea things.

'You said hello to your father yet, son?' Mary asked Jonathan, while she watched what Rose was doing from the corner of her eye.

'Dad is here?' Jonathan said, sounding surprised. 'I thought he was in America on business.'

'He came back last night. Brought some woman with him. She's staying the weekend, so he tells me. She's already making all sorts of demands as if she owns the place. Get the rooms all opened up! Send to the village for more staff! She won't believe me when I tell her that we can manage perfectly well. She's already wrapped Mrs Hammond around her little finger by saying she needs more help. Well, that's your father for you. There's nothing like an old fool.'

A bell jangled furiously. Mary glanced to her left where a row of old-fashioned bells hung in a row. 'That's her. Probably looking for her afternoon tea in the sitting room.' Mary began to heave herself out of her chair. 'I suppose I'd better get a tray sorted for them.'

'You just stay where you are, Mary. They can wait a moment or two.' Jonathan squatted on his heels next to the old woman. 'Maybe they're right. More help would make life a lot easier for you. I thought you had people in from the village during the day? Where are they?'

'Oh, they're away home. They only do the cleaning. Said that's all they're paid for. And they're right. Mrs Hammond wants to get another cook, someone who's lighter on their feet. Someone who's younger and can manage to take trays up and down all day.' Mary folded her arms and her face took on a mutinous look. 'I'm not going anywhere. I've been here all my life and the only way anyone's going to get me out of here is in a wooden box.'

Although Rose's heart went out to the older woman, she had to hide a smile. She was getting the distinct impression that no one was able to make Mary do anything she didn't want to. This Mrs Hammond, whoever she was, sounded like a sergeant-major. And as for Lord Cavendish's friend, she sounded as if she'd be better off at the Ritz.

'Tell you what, why don't you and Jonathan have your tea and a chat? If you tell me how to fix the tray, I'll take it upstairs for you. I'll introduce myself while I'm at it. And while I'm away, you can tell Jonathan about those chest pains you've been having.'

'How did you know? I mean, what chest pains? There's nothing wrong with me.'

'Yes, there is,' Rose said gently. 'I saw the way you were rubbing your chest when you got up a few moments ago. And you seem a little short of breath. It's probably nothing, but worth getting checked out.' She pretended to look fierce. 'Especially if, as you say, you plan to stick around for a few years yet.'

'Now, Mary. Why didn't you tell me?' Jonathan said, frowning. 'You know I would have come to see you long before now if I'd thought you needed me.'

'Take no notice of Rose. She doesn't know what she's talking about.' But something in their expressions must have told her that further protests would be a waste of time. 'Oh, well, then, if you have to have a look, go on. But don't you go saying anything to anyone, mind.'

While Jonathan returned to the cottage to fetch his stethoscope, Rose laid the tray under Mary's guidance. 'Just point me in the right direction. I'll be back as soon as I've handed this over.'

'It's the third door on the right at the stop of the stairs.' She paused and her mouth lifted in a smile. 'And if you could tell Lady Muck or whatever her name is that there has never been dandelion tea in my kitchen as long as I've been cook and there's no way it will ever be served here as long as I've breath in my body, I'd appreciate it.'

Rose carried the tray up the sweeping staircase until she got to the top. She smiled to herself. Now waitress was being added to her list of jobs.

She found the room she was looking for. The

door was open, so she coughed and entered. A man got to his feet and instantly she recognised Jonathan's father from his photograph. He shared the same arrogant nose and wide mouth as well as thick brown hair with his son.

'Hello?' Lord Cavendish raised an eyebrow. 'You must be new. I don't think I've met you before.' His voice was welcoming, but more than that, to her chagrin, Rose was aware of his eyes sweeping across her body in the most disconcerting way.

'Just leave the tray over there.' The woman who had been looking out the window turned and waved at Rose with a dismissive hand. She was considerably younger than Lord Cavendish, closer to Rose's age, possibly a year or two older.

'I'm not new,' Rose said, placing the tray on a coffee table in front of the sofa. 'I'm here with Jonathan. He's having a look at Mary downstairs. She's not feeling too great, so I offered to bring the tray up for her.'

Lord Cavendish's eyes clouded with concern and something else—could it be surprise?

'Jonathan is here? To see Mary? Why didn't she say she was feeling unwell? I'll go and see her myself.' He hurried out of the room, leaving Rose alone with his guest.

'I'm Rose Taylor,' Rose introduced herself. Cool grey eyes swept over her and this time Rose could tell Lord Cavendish's guest was taking in her clothes, her haircut, assessing the cost and then wondering what on earth she was doing with the son of a lord.

'I work with Jonathan. I'm his nurse.' Now, why had she said that? It was none of this woman's business.

The grey eyes narrowed and she nodded to herself as if something had been cleared up.

'How do you do, Miss Taylor?' The voice was as cool as the eyes and Rose noticed she didn't bother to introduce herself. 'Did cook manage to rustle up some dandelion tea? She certainly had enough time.'

Hadn't this woman taken in a thing Rose had said? For the first time in her life she found herself detesting someone on sight.

'I'm afraid Mary isn't feeling well,' she said stiffly. 'Now, if you'll excuse me, I'll leave you to your tea.'

She found Jonathan and his father deep in

conversation. Rose could sense the strained atmosphere between father and son.

'Mary needs to rest, Father. For at least a week, possibly longer.'

'And I've tried to tell her that on more than one occasion, but she won't listen to me.'

'When did you tell her? You've hardly been here over the last six months,' Jonathan said sharply. The two men noticed Rose and stopped their conversation abruptly.

'Father, can I introduce Rose Taylor? Rose, this is my father, Lord Cavendish.' Rose suppressed the inane desire to curtsy.

'I apologise for my lack of manners upstairs,' he said. 'I was anxious to check on Mary myself and to see my son. Who...' he shot a look in Jonathan's direction '...hasn't seen fit to visit for quite some time.'

'Now is not the time or place, Father,' Jonathan said warningly. It was the first time Rose had seen him look so grim. Something was clearly badly wrong between father and son.

'You are quite right, Jonathan. Now, if you'll both excuse me, I'd better find Mrs Hammond and see what can be done to find someone to fill in for Mary while she's resting.'

As soon as he had left, Rose turned to Jonathan. His normal open and cheerful expression was tight. 'How is she?'

'I think she has mild ischaemic heart disease. I want to arrange to have her admitted to hospital for proper tests, but she's not keen. But I've threatened to call an ambulance if she doesn't agree. Father's right. I should have called in here more often, especially when he's away.'

'Look, why don't you make some calls, and I'll go and check on Mary? Add my voice to yours if you think it would make a difference.'

'I'm sorry to have got you mixed up in this.' He grinned ruefully. 'So much for me trying to give you a relaxing day out away from work.'

He looked so regretful Rose's heart went out to him.

'I don't mind being mixed up in this, as you put it. Isn't that what friends are for? To help each other?'

Jonathan looked perplexed. 'Is it?' he said thoughtfully. 'I wouldn't know. I can't say I've ever had to rely on my friends before. They're always there when I need to let off steam and that's all I ever expected from them.' He smiled down at her. 'You're a good person, Rose Taylor. You know that, don't you?'

Ah, well, Rose thought dismally. It was good that Jonathan knew she was his friend—even if he didn't want her as his lover.

She found Mary right at the top of the house, several flights up. The older woman was sitting at the window, looking out at the garden. She folded her arms across her chest and glared at Rose.

'If you have come up here to try and persuade me to go into hospital, you're wasting your time. And you can tell Master Jonathan that from me.' She pursed her lips.

'You will probably only have to go in for a night, two at the most. Just while they do some tests. Then you can come back here, although I'm going to suggest that you move to a room that doesn't require quite as many stairs.'

'There's nowt wrong with this room. I've been in here since the day I started work thirty years ago and I see no reason to move now.' She blinked furiously, but she couldn't quite disguise the moisture in her eyes.

'What is it, Mary? What's truly worrying you? Come on, you can tell me.'

'If I leave here, I'll never come back. That woman down there with Lord Cavendish will persuade him to employ someone younger. I know she will. She's only been here a couple of days and already I can see that's she's imagining herself as the next Lady Cavendish.'

So that was what was worrying the old woman. Somehow Rose knew that Jonathan would never let that happen.

'This place is as much my home as anyone's. I don't have anywhere else to go. The only way I want to leave here is in a box.'

'How long have you been hiding your symptoms, Mary?'

'A month, maybe two. I thought it was indigestion at first. Then the pain started to get worse whenever I had to climb the stairs, so I knew it must be my heart.'

'Why didn't you call Jonathan? You must have known he'd be concerned enough to come and see you straight away.'

'Oh, he's got enough on his plate without me bothering him with my little problems. Anyway...' she leaned across and dropped her voice to a conspiratorial whisper. 'I can't make myself believe he's actually a doctor. Not the boy I've watched grow up. It doesn't seem right somehow.'

Rose pulled up a seat and sat down.

'You seem very fond of him,' she said.

'The poor mite was only little when his mother died. I'm probably the nearest, most constant person he had in his life as a child. Whenever he was home from school, he'd spend more time at the kitchen table with me than upstairs. When he wasn't running around outside, that was.'

'What about Lord Cavendish?'

'He was distraught when Jonathan's mother died. But his way of dealing with it was to throw himself into work. He couldn't see that Jonathan needed him more than ever. Then six months after Jonathan's mother died, Lord Cavendish returned from an overseas trip married to the second Lady Cavendish. That didn't last too long. He divorced the third wife a year or so ago, and now it looks as if he's preparing to marry again.'

'His fourth marriage?' Rose couldn't keep the shock from her voice. 'Surely that's a little excessive?'

'Ah, well. He always did have an eye for the women.' She moved her gaze back to the window and her eyes glistened. 'I don't think he's ever got over the first Lady Cavendish. Now, she was a real lady. Not in the sense of being from aristocracy, you understand, her own background was quite humble, but in terms of knowing how to treat people.' She pointed a gnarled finger to the floor. 'That woman will never compete in a hundred years.'

There was a tap at the door and Jonathan walked into the room. With a guilty start, Rose realised she had been gossiping.

'How's my favourite girl, then?' Jonathan said. 'Has Rose managed to talk you into going to the hospital?'

Before Mary had a chance to protest, Rose interrupted smoothly. 'I think Mary will agree to go to the hospital. She's just a wee bit worried that your father will replace her while she's away.'

It looked as if a thundercloud had descended on Jonathan's face. 'Whatever gave you that idea? I agree you could do with more help, but no one is thinking of replacing you. This house would fall down without you to look after it—and us. You've been here as long as I can remember. It's your home, Mary. Don't ever forget that.'

Mary looked relieved but then her mouth puckered. 'But it's not just to do with you, Master Jonathan, is it? At least, not for some time. Right now your father makes the decisions, and if he marries again, it'll be the new Lady Cavendish's wishes that take precedence.'

'My father might have his faults, Mary, Lord knows, but he'll never agree to replacing you.' His eyes narrowed. 'I had no idea he was planning to marry again.'

'Now, don't you go saying anything,' Mary protested. 'It's not official yet. At least, he's not said as much. It's just I heard his guest speaking on the phone. She was telling them not to make plans for the summer because she was planning a big party.'

Jonathan's lips thinned. 'You leave my father to me, Mary. Come on, I'm going to drive you to the hospital. They're expecting us. If you want to get a few things together, I'll let my father know what's happening.' He turned to Rose. 'I can't apologise enough, but there's only room in my car for Mary and I. If I ask my father to take you to the railway station, would you manage to find your own way home from there?'

'Of course. Really, it's no problem.' She smiled. 'It's far more important that Mary gets investigated, and the sooner the better.' She got to her feet. 'We'll leave you alone to pack your things, Mary. Take your time. There's no rush.'

Jonathan still looked livid when they left Mary. 'I need to go and find my father. It shouldn't take too long. Would you like to wait down-stairs?'

'I think I'll take a stroll in the garden while I'm waiting. And if it's inconvenient for your father to take me to the station, perhaps you can call me a taxi?'

'He'll take you,' Jonathan responded grimly. 'One thing you can say about my father is that his manners are impeccable.'

The grounds of the hall were as lavish as the inside. Rose kept close to the house in case she was needed. To her right, a small rose-coloured archway invited her to explore. She dipped her head and entered a small hidden garden. She gasped with pleasure. Someone had taken the time to make this little spot less formal than the rest of the gardens. It was a mass of flowers and the smell of rosemary, lavender and mint drifted up her nostrils. Seeing a bench with views out to the open hills off to one side, Rose took a seat and closed her eyes.

Something was badly wrong between Jonathan and his father. She wondered if he'd have taken her to the house, or even to the gatehouse, if he'd known his father was at home. Somehow she felt sure he wouldn't have. How could someone not get on with their father? Especially when he was the only family member Jonathan had left. Rose couldn't remember ever having cross words with her parents.

She was beginning to realise that Jonathan was a much more complex man than she had ever imagined and she knew that every moment she spent with him she was falling deeper and deeper in love. The realisation was not a welcome one.

Voices drifted from the open window behind her. She recognised Jonathan's and his father's. Both men sounded heated.

'How can you think of marrying yet again?' Jonathan's voice was raised.

'What I choose to do with my life is none of your goddamn business. And speaking of marriage, when are you going to stop seducing every woman on the planet and get into a real relationship? You can't carry on the way you do for the rest of your life. At some point you're going to accept you have responsibilities.'

'That's rich, coming from you.'

Rose got to her feet. The last thing she wanted was to overhear the argument between father and son. She started to edge away from the window.

'What about that prissy little thing you brought with you? She looks like she has a sensible head. Why, for God's sake, can't you find someone like her to settle down with?'

Rose froze in mid-stride. This was so embarrassing. How dare Lord Cavendish refer to her as prissy? Even if she supposed there was an element of truth in the description. But she had to admit she was dying to know how Jonathan would respond.

'Rose? As the future Lady Cavendish?' Jonathan laughed harshly. 'Now you mention it, she'd be a lot more suitable than the last two *you* chose to marry. At least she has brains and a kind heart under that prissy exterior, as you call it. I can tell you she's worth a hundred of the women you married after Mother.'

Lord Cavendish dropped his voice and Rose could hear the sadness and regret in it. 'Why are we always arguing, son? You know I need your help. I'm not getting any younger and running my businesses as well as this estate is getting too much.'

'Are you all right? You've not being feeling ill, have you? When did you last have a check-up?' This time it was Jonathan's voice that was full of concern. Despite their earlier angry words, Rose could tell the two men cared about one another.

'I'm fine. I promise. I'd feel a lot better if I knew that you were settling down. You can't keep on living the way you do. God, man, your name is in the paper every other day. Always with a different woman. You need to get married—have children. I need to know before I die that there is going to be someone to carry on the family line.'

'You're a fine person to talk.' The anger was back in Jonathan's voice. 'Is that why you married Mother? Just to provide an heir for the future? My God, didn't you love her at all?'

'Love her? Of course I loved her. She was the best thing that ever happened to me.'

'Which is why you married again within six months of her death.'

Rose couldn't bear to hear any more. She tiptoed away until she could no longer hear the voices and waited by the front door of the house. She was tingling as she recalled the words Jonathan had used to describe her. Kind and clever. Well, she hoped she was. But she would have liked to hear herself described as beautiful and sexy as well, even if it was untrue. This way she felt like Jonathan's sister and that wasn't how she wanted him to see her at all. She wanted someone to find her exciting and interesting. She wanted *Jonathan* to find her exciting and interesting. If she didn't have a future, she wanted a here and now. And why not? Where had playing safe got her? She felt her blood heat her veins. Prissy. She'd give them prissy. She could be as exciting and interesting as the next woman and with a bit of help—possibly a lot of help—she could do sexy as well. It was as if she'd been sleeping up until the moment she'd realised her life could

be snatched away at any time. Now she wanted
to wake up and experience life before it was too
late. And who better to show her that life than
Jonathan Cavendish? After all, it wasn't as if she
could break his heart.

CHAPTER SEVEN

'I CAN'T wait for it! Do you think there'll be loads of celebrities there?' Jenny was practically bouncing out of her chair with excitement. Jonathan had informed everyone that he was taking a table at the annual fundraising ball and they were all invited. It had been on the tip of Rose's tongue to refuse, but instead she had found herself agreeing. What harm could it do? And it was one more thing to add to her list. Besides, it was another opportunity to be with Jonathan outside work and although she knew she was storing up heartache for the future, she couldn't bring herself to deny herself a moment of him.

'I get the feeling there will be one or two.' Rose had to smile at Jenny's enthusiasm.

'We'll have to go shopping for something to wear,' Jenny said. 'And you'll have to go to the hairdresser.' She pulled out her mobile. 'You must go to mine. He's fantastic. He'll know exactly what to do with your hair.'

'What's wrong with my hair?' Rose protested. She eyed her colleague doubtfully, recalling the spiky hairdo she usually sported outside her job. If Jenny thought she was going to go punk, she had another think coming.

Jenny looked at Rose thoughtfully. 'I would die for hair like yours. It's just a little old-fashioned, you know. It could do with an update. In fact, and I don't mean to be rude or anything, the whole of you could do with an update.' She wrinkled her nose. 'That cardigan you're so fond of wearing, for example. That has to go.'

'Hey, there's nothing wrong with it. It's warm and comfortable,' Rose protested.

'And makes it seem as if you're wearing a sack. Come on, Rose. You don't want to look like someone's maiden aunt. Not when all those glamorous people are going to be there.' She held up her hand, cutting Rose's protests off. 'You will not let the side down. I simply won't allow it.'

Dowdy? Someone's maiden aunt? Now she had two more derogatory adjectives to add to the steadily growing list. Up until recently nobody had ever complained about the way she looked. Or complimented her either, she had to admit. But she hadn't minded. Hadn't she always told herself that external appearances weren't important? But this was the new Rose, she reminded herself. The one who was determined to break out of her shell. Hadn't she promised herself to try different things? And if that included a new image, so be it.

By Saturday afternoon, Rose had been done to within an inch of her life. Jenny's hairdresser had cut her hair into a sharp modern style while keeping it long. He had parted it to one side and now it fell over one side of her face. If she had to keep blowing out little puffs of hair so she could see what she was doing—as Jenny had said, what did it matter if she looked chic and alluring? But the hair over her eyes wasn't the only thing obscuring her vision. Jenny had insisted that no way was she allowed to wear her glasses. She had marched her to the optician and Rose was now trying contact lenses. She finally managed to get them in and blinked furiously as water streamed from her eyes. She'd give them until she had to apply her make-up and if they hadn't settled it was on with the glasses. The last thing she needed was to turn up looking like she had spent the day crying.

She and Jenny had been shopping for a dress and eventually, after what had seemed like hours of tramping around London, had settled on a silky, two-tone red number that shimmered as Rose walked.

'Wow! I had no idea you had a figure like that underneath those dreadful clothes you insist on wearing,' Jenny had said. 'I could diet for a year and still not have a body like that. Why on earth do you cover it up?'

'I'm too thin,' Rose had said. 'I hate the way my bones stick out all over the place. They used to call me pin legs when I was in school. Someone even accused me of being anorexic.' The memory brought painful feelings flooding back. At school she had been teased for being too thin and she had never lost that gawky, unattractive feeling. Now all the worries and anxieties about the way she looked seemed so petty and pointless. And Jenny was right. The dress did amazing things to her figure. The way it hung, the way it moved when she moved. For the first time in her life, Rose felt glamorous.

'And don't even think you're going to get out of buying new underwear,' Jenny had said. 'Are these mum pants or what?'

'There is nothing wrong with my underwear,' Rose protested. 'Okay, they might be serviceable rather than sexy, but who is going to see?'

'Seeing, as you put it, isn't really the point. At least not all of it. If you don't feel sexy under your clothes, how are you going to look sexy?'

Rose had to laugh. She let Jenny steer her to the lingerie department and allowed her to bully her into buying several lacy bras with matching panties. Rose dreaded to think what her credit-card bill was going to be like. But she had to admit she had plenty money in the bank and it was fun. It was the first time she could remember that she had spent so much money on herself. After all, she reminded herself with a stab, who knew if she would ever have the opportunity to dress up like this again? And right now saving her pennies for a rainy day seemed like an exercise in futility. One thing her illness had done was to free her from the small pointless worries of everyday life.

As she finished putting the finishing touches

to her make-up, almost the way the girl at the cosmetics counter had shown her, she had to admit that now she was as far away from prissy as it was possible to be. She giggled. All she needed was a cigarette holder in one hand and a glass of champagne in the other, and she'd look like Mata Hari, even though she didn't smoke. And while the contacts had settled, she was sure the famous seductress hadn't blinked quite so often.

She sashayed down the stairs, revelling in the feel of the soft fabric of her dress against her skin.

Her father glanced up when she entered the sitting room and attempted a wolf whistle.

'Can this really be my little girl?' he said, his eyes glistening. 'So grown up and so beautiful?'

Over the last couple of weeks his condition had continued to improve. He was getting about fairly easily with one stick and his speech was less slurred. He was able to manage more of the activities of daily living by himself, even if it still took him twice as long as it used to. Being more independent had cheered him up enormously and Rose knew that soon her parents would be able to cope without her. It lifted some of the burden from her shoulders when she thought about what the future could bring— for them as well as her.

'Yes, Dad. I know it's hard to believe.' She whirled around. 'I find it hard to believe too.'

'I've never seen you so lit up,' her mother said quietly. 'Is it just the night out or is there another reason why you're glowing inside and out?' Rose had made sure her mother didn't see her torment and worry. Around her mother, she forced herself to think only about things that made her happy. Like Jonathan.

He had insisted on sending a car for her. She had tried to protest, saying she'd be quite happy to take the tube, but he had been adamant.

'You and the rest of the gang are my guests. There is no way I'm going to let you arrive on foot.' He had smiled down at her and her heart banged against her ribs. 'Just give in gracefully, kid. For once.'

But she hadn't expected to find him at her door. He looked jaw-droppingly handsome in his dinner suit and bow-tie. When he saw her, he looked taken aback. He bowed briefly from the waist. Then he whistled. 'You look absolutely stunning,' he said. 'Have you had your hair cut? It suits you.' Rose felt a wave of pleasure wash over her. Perhaps he was just being polite, but the look in his eyes told her he meant ever word.

'You don't look so bad yourself,' she quipped.

'I'll just wish your parents good evening,' Jonathan said, stepping inside the small hallway. He was so close she could smell the faint scent of his shampoo and the familiar spice of his aftershave. He touched her briefly on her shoulder and a shiver ran down her spine. 'There are going to be a few women there tonight with their noses severely out of joint. You do know that, don't you?' His breath was like a caress on her skin.

After a few brief words with her parents, he ushered Rose out to the waiting car.

Inside the stretch limousine was an over-excited Jenny, as well as Vicki and her husband. It was another new experience for Rose. There were seats along one side as well as a small bar. Jonathan reached into the bar and brought out a chilled bottle of champagne, which he popped with a flourish. When everyone had their glasses filled he toasted them. 'I hope you all have a great time tonight and remember it's all for a good cause.'

'I'm so glad you could manage,' Rose said to Vicki after she had introduced her husband, Russell. 'How are you feeling?'

'Much better. I don't know how long I'll last, but I couldn't miss it. It's my favourite night of the year. The one and only night I really get to let my hair down.'

Vicki, who had declined the champagne in favour of fresh orange juice, waved her glass at Jonathan. 'Are you going to be auctioned as usual tonight?'

'Not if I can help it,' Jonathan replied. 'I made a deal with the organisers this year. They've agreed I don't have to take part as long as I match the highest bid for one of the other guests.'

'Auctioned?' Jenny said, sounding puzzled. 'What do you mean?'

'Every year at this do they ask some of the eligible bachelors to agree to auction a date. They have to parade up and down a catwalk while women bid for a date with them. It can get quite heated. At least, it did last year,' Vicki replied, grinning.

'What happened?'

Jonathan was frowning at Vicki, shaking his head from side to side. But she wasn't to be deterred.

'It almost caused a riot. The organiser made Jonathan remove his jacket and shirt. He was allowed to leave his bow-tie on. Not that that gave him much to hide behind.' Vicki chuckled. Jonathan was looking mortified.

Rose almost spluttered into her champagne. The image of a semi-naked Jonathan strolling down a catwalk was almost too much.

'Who won?' Jenny asked.

'That was the best part. It was one of the elderly matrons. You should have seen her excitement when she learned her bid was the highest.'

Everyone, even Jonathan, laughed. 'She actually bought the date for her daughter. I don't know who was more embarrassed, her or me. Still, we had a pleasant enough meal. But I will never do that again. No way. Uhuh.'

By this time they were pulling up outside the hotel where the dinner-dance was to be held. Although the hotel was famous, Rose had never been inside before.

As they climbed out of the car, they were swarmed by photographers.

'Look this way, Jonathan,' they called out. She pulled back inside the car. She hadn't expected this. There was no way she wanted to be photographed, even if it wasn't her they were after.

But she had reckoned without Jonathan. As the rest of the group made their way into the hotel, he jumped back into the car and pulled the door closed.

'What's wrong?' he asked.

'I don't want to go out there,' Rose whispered. 'I hate having my photograph taken.'

'I don't much like it either,' Jonathan replied, 'but the best way to cope with it is to pose for a couple of photographs and then walk away.'

'I can't.' Rose shook her head.

'Yes, you can,' Jonathan said firmly. 'They are going to want a picture of the amazingly beautiful woman who has arrived with me.' He looked regretful. 'I'm an idiot. If I had thought for one minute that you'd hate the attention, I would have arrived separately. But it's too late now. The more you hide away, the more curious they're going to be. There's nothing else for it. We have to brave the lions in their den.' He grinned. 'Just follow my lead and it'll be over in a few minutes. Okay?'

Rose nodded and, head held high, stepped out of the car. Once again, there was an explosion of blinding flashes.

'Who is your lady friend, Jonathan? Is it serious? Are you settling down?'

Rose's heart sank as she realised that her climbing back into the car had only made matters worse. Now they thought she was someone.

'Hey, guys, give us a break.' Jonathan kept his tone even. 'Ms Taylor is just one of several guests I have with me this evening.'

'Does this mean your relationship with Jessamine Goldsmith is over?' another reporter asked.

'Ms Goldsmith and I are good friends and have never been anything more.'

'So there's no truth that she dumped you because you refused to name the day?'

'None at all. Now, if you'll excuse us,' Jonathan replied smoothly, 'I have guests waiting inside.'

'Could you tell us a bit about yourself, Ms Taylor?' Another reporter thrust his microphone into Rose's face and she almost stumbled. As quick as a flash, Jonathan reached out to steady her with one hand while with the other took hold of the microphone and pushed it away. 'Just carry on walking,' he said into her ear. 'I'll keep them busy.'

'It's okay,' Rose replied, lifting her head again. 'I can deal with this.' She took a deep breath and turned to the journalists with the biggest smile she could manage. 'I'm afraid there isn't much to tell. I work with Dr Cavendish. I'm his practice nurse. As he's told you, I'm one of a party of his staff. Now, I know that you are all interested in what this evening is in aid of. Perhaps you'd like me to bring you up to speed with the work of the charity?'

From the corner of her eye she saw the look of surprise on Jonathan's face, followed by a look of approval. She had made a point of looking the charity up on the Internet during a quiet spell at the clinic. She carried on, inching her way towards the hotel door as she briefly outlined the work of the charity, making sure that she kept smiling. Fortunately it seemed to work. As soon as another car pulled up at the kerb, the reporters turned away to catch the new arrival.

Inside, Jonathan was immediately surrounded by people. Rose left him to greet his friends and acquaintances, and spying Jenny and Victoria from the corner of her eye went over to their table. Jenny's eyes were alive with excitement.

'I've already spotted at least ten famous people,' she told Rose. 'Everywhere I look there is someone whose face I recognise. Isn't this brilliant? I can hardly believe I'm here.' She pointed across the room. 'I saw her film last week. Isn't she beautiful? Even more than she is in her films? And as for that dress, isn't it to die for?'

It was overwhelming. Rose felt drab and shy in the presence of so many well-known people, all of whom looked relaxed and confident. In the crowd she noticed Lady Hilton. Although she had a smile painted on her face, Rose could tell instantly, even from a distance, that she was worried. When she thought no one was looking her smile disappeared, to be replaced with lines of worry around her mouth and eyes. Forgetting her shyness, Rose made her way through the throng until she was by her side.

'Lady Hilton,' she murmured in her ear. 'Are you okay?'

'My dear girl, I didn't know you were coming. It's lovely to see you.' She raised her face for Rose to kiss. Although the older woman's voice was bright, she didn't fool Rose.

'How is Lord Hilton?' she asked quietly.

'Much the same as when you last saw him, my dear.'

As promised, Rose had been making regular trips to their estate to check up on Lord Hilton.

'He insisted I come tonight, even though I told him I'd rather stay with him. But he wouldn't hear of it. He said that the Hiltons had never missed this fundraiser in twenty years and we weren't going to start now.' Sophia smiled wanly. 'You know how much we both owe you, don't you, dear? Without your help we would never have been able to keep him at home. Jonathan's a lucky man. Goodall is with Giles tonight. I'll stay until the auction then I'll go home.' She glanced around the room. 'Where is Jonathan? I'd like to speak to him.' Her voice regained some of its familiar strength.

It was kind of Sophia to think Jonathan was lucky to have her as a nurse. But Rose knew that the small help she had been able to give the couple had made a difference to the dark days they were facing. It had helped her too. There was a bitter-sweet poignancy in helping the couple through their last days together.

'Why don't you join us at our table?' Rose suggested. Then felt immediately embarrassed. Lady Hilton was bound to have friends to sit with. But, to her surprise, Sophia looked relieved.

'Thank you, my dear. I'd like that. It would save me having to answer questions about my Giles. Everyone means to be kind, but it gets a little difficult.'

'Come on, then.' Rose smiled. 'Let's get you seated and you can rest your feet. Vicki and her husband are at our table too. I'm sure she'd like to see you.'

Lady Hilton seemed glad to see Vicki. Jenny, on the other hand, was struck dumb for the first time Rose could remember. Rose suppressed a smile when Jenny attempted a small curtsy when she was introduced to Lady Hilton, and then, realising what she had done, blushed to the roots of her hair.

'Apparently the auction is going to start before dinner and continue all the way through,' Vicki told everyone at the table. 'There's a list of what's being auctioned under the menu.'

Rose picked up the bound, heavy pages of the auction items. There were cars and weeks on private islands, trips on personal Lear jets, diamonds, paintings and—she smiled—the date with one of London's eligible bachelors. That must be the event Jonathan had told them about. She wished there was something she could afford to bid on, but there was nothing she could afford. She would have to sit back and watch the fun.

'Are you bidding on anything, my dear? I think I'll make an offer on one of the paintings. I usually do and then slip it back into the auction the following year. We have far too many paintings as it is.'

'I'm afraid there is nothing here I can afford,' Rose admitted.

'Lady Hilton, Sophia, what an unexpected pleasure.' Jonathan's voice came from behind her. 'And to have you sit with us is a double honour.'

'I haven't taken your seat, have I?' Lady Hilton. 'If I have, I can easily return to my own table. I'm sure Rose would rather sit next to you than an old lady like me.' Her eyes slid to Rose and the sadness was replaced with a twinkle. 'Doesn't she look beautiful?'

'Yes, she does,' Jonathan replied quietly. 'Easily the most beautiful woman in the room.'

Rose felt a blush steal up her cheeks. But she knew better than to take his words seriously. No doubt it was the way he spoke to all women.

'Unfortunately, I won't be needing my seat for the next hour. Despite my best efforts, Lady Somerville has roped me into the bachelor date auction. She won't take no for an answer.'

Rose stifled a giggle. It was the first time she had seen him look ill at ease.

'Isn't that the thing you were telling us about in the car? The one you said you would never do again?' Jenny leant over, dragging her eyes away from the seemingly endless parade of actresses, models and pop stars.

Jonathan sighed heavily. 'I tried to tell her that I'd match the highest amount bid for any of the men in the auction, but she wouldn't hear of it. She says she needs me to make the numbers up, and I was the highest earner last year.'

'If I had the money, I'd bid for you,' Jenny said stoutly.

'Just remember it's all for a good cause,' Lady Hilton reminded Jonathan.

A woman was waving frantically from the other side of the room, trying to get his attention.

'Looks like I'm up. Wish me luck, everyone.' Then, with a last rueful grimace, Jonathan left them.

'You should bid for him,' Lady Hilton told Rose. 'He could do with a good woman. Someone to settle him down. I know his father worries about him.'

Rose was mortified. Jonathan and her? It was inconceivable. Lady Hilton should know that.

'I hardly think Jonathan and I are suited,' she said, keeping her voice mild.

'Why ever not? Don't you find him good looking and charming? He'll inherit a title when his father dies. Half the women in this room would jump at the chance to be the future Lady Cavendish.' She peered after Jonathan. 'What's wrong with him?'

'There's nothing wrong with him.' Rose wished the floor would open up and swallow her. 'It's just that I'm hardly suited to being the lady of the manor, am I?' And if that wasn't bad enough, she had no future to offer any man. But she wasn't going to talk about that.

'Rubbish, girl. If you think just because you're a commoner, and he belongs to aristocracy, think again. His mother, the current Lord Cavendish's first wife, was a commoner too. Things are changing. And for the better, I would say.' She looked thoughtful for a moment. 'I don't think his father ever got over the death of his first wife. She was the love of his life.'

'What happened to her?'

'She died when Jonathan was five. Pneumonia, would you believe? The poor mite was devastated. His father sent him away to boarding school just when Jonathan needed him most. I don't think Jonathan has ever forgiven him and I suspect he blames him for not noticing how unwell Clara was. How can a child understand that Cavendish sending him away was nothing to do with him? That his father just couldn't cope? The sight of him every day was just too much of a painful reminder. It was the way things were done. I'm not saying it was right. Then his father married again. Within six months. I think it was because he was lonely, but Jonathan never forgave him for that either.'

It explained the tension and anger between Jonathan and his father.

'Why didn't Lord Cavendish explain? Tell his son how he felt?'

Lady Hilton looked surprised. 'Men don't speak of these things, my dear. At least, not then. Oh, I know these days it's the done thing to talk about your feelings, endlessly. But that isn't the way Jonathan and his father were brought up.'

Rose felt a pang for the child Jonathan had been. How terrible to lose your mother and then to be sent away into a strange environment from the only home you had known. What would that do to a grieving child? At least she had always been surrounded by the love of her parents and had always known that they would do anything for her happiness.

There was no more time to talk as everyone was instructed to take their seats by a tall woman with short, platinum-blonde hair.

'That's Mrs Tenant, Rose.' Lady Hilton whispered. 'She used to be a model in the sixties. Her father was enormously wealthy. Perhaps even wealthier than Lord Cavendish. She married for love and she's been blissfully happy. She helps Lady Somerville run the auction. I have to say, between them, they've helped raise hundreds of thousands of pounds over the years.'

Mrs Tenant—Julia—welcomed everyone in a rich Yorkshire accent that was as far away from the plush London tones all around her as it was possible to be.

'We are going to start with the eligible bachelors' auction,' she said after she had spoken briefly about the charity. 'I know this is a favourite event for most of you. Now, we have five men, all single and all looking forward to their dates with the lucky women who win the auction. Don't be mean, anyone. Dig deep into those pockets.'

Everyone settled down, looking towards the runway that had been erected near the front of the room. A hush descended as Julia introduced the first 'bachelor'—a British tennis player who had been taking the country by storm over the last year. He swaggered onto the stage in a pair of tennis shorts and nothing else, looking, Rose thought, extremely self-conscious with a nervous grin on his face. There were a number of wolf whistles as he walked to the edge of the stage and flexed his forearm in a way that had become familiar to millions of tennis fans around the world.

'Who'll start the bidding? Come on, now, ladies, don't be shy. Who'll give me a hundred pounds?'

A sea of arms shot up. 'A hundred and fifty,' came a call from the back. Rose swivelled around in her seat to find a young woman waving her arms in the air, a bundle of notes in each hand.

'Two hundred,' came another voice. Soon the bidding was up to four hundred and after Julia had promised that the player was throwing in a couple of prime seats for Wimbledon in June, the bidding rose to five hundred pounds before the triumphant girl who had started the bidding won her date.

Three others followed in quick succession. Rose felt sorry for the aristocrat with an unfortunate smile who only managed to raise two hundred pounds and she suspected his mother was behind that.

Jonathan was last to take the stage. He had, or someone had made him, remove his shirt. He strolled up the runway in his dinner trousers, bow-tie and jacket, his exposed chest smooth and muscular. If he felt self-conscious no one would have known from his confident grin. Rose felt a shiver run down her spine. He really was the sexiest man she had ever known.

The bidding started at three hundred pounds and quickly rose to five hundred.

'Come on, ladies. You can do better than that. Jonathan is one of London's most eligible bachelors. As far as I'm aware, there is no one in his life at the moment.'

The bidding rose by another hundred pounds. And even further. Suddenly, Lady Hilton's hand shot up. 'One thousand pounds,' she said firmly. Rose looked at the old lady in astonishment and was even more surprised when she received a saucy wink in response.

'One thousand pounds. Sold to Lady Hilton,' Julia said with a flourish. 'A new record.'

As she thanked everyone and the music faded away, Jenny and Vicki turned surprised faces towards Lady Hilton, who leaned closer to Rose and whispered in a conspiratorial voice, 'I bought him for you, dear.'

'Me?' Rose squeaked, thinking that Lady Hilton had lost her marbles. 'Whatever for?'

She leaned over and took Rose's hand in one of hers. 'Because I think you're right for each other, that's why. Even if he can't see it yet.'

Lady Hilton hadn't a clue how wrong she was. Rose was hardly the catch of the century. Even if she didn't have an uncertain future, unable to have children, bookish, what would anyone ever see in her? Let alone a man like Jonathan, who had dated some of the most beautiful and confident women in the world? Her heart stumbled. She'd enjoyed Jonathan's company over the last few weeks. More than enjoyed it, but soon it would be over. She'd be leaving, going back to her life in Edinburgh, whatever she decided to do about the operation. Her empty life, she thought miserably. She had been happy with it once, but that had been before Jonathan. Now she knew, however long she lived, her life would be lonely and grey without him.

Jonathan, who had replaced his shirt, slipped into the chair beside her. 'Thank God, that's over,' he said. 'I think I might just make my excuses for next year. But thank you, Sophia, for making the winning bid. Where would you like me to take you? Horseracing? To a polo match? I know you love both.'

Lady Hilton smiled wryly. 'As much as I'd like to go somewhere with you, Jonathan, I rather suspect that this will be my last outing for a while.' She turned her head to the side, but not before Rose saw a tear slip down her cheek. 'That's why I've passed my date on to Rose here. I know she's been working hard. Not least as she keeps popping in to see how we are, bless her. And I don't think polo or the racecourse is altogether what's needed. I need you to come up with something much more…' she hesitated. 'Appropriate for Rose.'

Rose was thoroughly embarrassed. Imagine Jonathan being tasked with taking her out as if she were a bag of shopping or a pet requiring to be walked. It was too much.

'There's no need at all to take me out,' she muttered into his ear. 'But perhaps we should pretend—as if it's ever going to happen—for Lady Hilton's sake?'

Jonathan grinned and Rose's heart pinged.

'I'm not one to back out of anything,' he said into her ear. She felt his warm breath on the nape of her neck and a delicious thrill ran down her spine. Goose-bumps prickled her arms, making her shiver. 'And I didn't have you down as a quitter either,' he continued. 'In the meantime…' he held out a hand '…shall we dance?'

Almost in a daze, Rose let him lead her to the dance floor. Thankfully she knew how to waltz. Memories of her father twirling her and her mother around their small sitting room to the music of Mozart and Strauss brought a lump to her throat. She had never dreamed she would be putting it into practice in such a setting.

Jonathan held her tightly. She could smell his aftershave and feel the hard muscles of his chest against her head. An image of his bare chest, tanned, defined muscles made her want to groan out loud. Who would have ever suspected he had a body like that? All that polo playing must help. She pushed the thought of heavily muscled thighs away before she became any more flustered.

She looked into his eyes. He looked back and her world tipped. Damn the man. Damn everything. Why did she have to go and fall for him? And why did she have to be facing an uncertain future? Why? Why? Why?

'You are the most beautiful woman in the room tonight and the most remarkable,' Jonathan whispered into her hair.

All at once, Rose had had enough. If Jonathan thought he could play games with her he had another think coming. No matter how she felt about him. *Particularly* because of how she felt about him.

She pulled away from him so she could see his face. 'What do you want from me, Jonathan?' she asked.

'What do you mean?' he asked as he whirled around the dance floor.

'I'm not the woman for you, believe me.'

He frowned. 'Don't you think I should be the judge of that? Believe me, Rose Taylor. You're exactly the woman for me.' He paused by a door leading outside and pulled her into the fresh evening air. The scent of climbing roses drifted up her nostrils, intoxicating her.

Jonathan's finger stroked her hair away from her face. 'I don't think you have any idea just how lovely you are.' He smiled. 'But it's not just the way you look, you're a very special woman, Rose. Don't you know that? I can't believe that no one has won your heart yet.' He frowned and a shadow passed across his face. 'Or has some-one? Of course. What an idiot I've been. There's bound to be someone back in Edinburgh, wait-ing for you. God, do you love him? Would you dump him? Come out with me instead?' His smile was warm and tender. 'I promise you, you won't regret it.'

Rose's head was swirling. There was nothing she wanted more right now than to tell him that there was no one else and, yes, she would go out with him. Every day for the rest of her life. However long that would be. But she couldn't. It wasn't fair to her or to him. All at once she knew he was falling in love with her and it made her heart soar, but she also knew she already cared too much to deny him the happy-ever-after ending he deserved.

'There's no future for us,' she said bleakly.

'So there is someone else.'

Rose hesitated. It would be easier to let him believe that. But she wasn't going to lie to him. Even if she couldn't tell him the truth.

'No, there isn't anyone.'

'In that case, I'm not going to take no for an answer. I owe you a date. And a date is what we're going to go on. Like it or not.' Although he smiled, Rose sensed the determination behind his words. And even though she knew she should avoid him, for his sake if not hers, she couldn't resist the temptation. Another memory. A few more moments with Jonathan to store away like a squirrel.

'Okay, then. If you insist, I'll go out with you. I guess it's not really a date anyway.' She tried to sound casual.

'Not really a date,' Jonathan muttered under his breath. 'If I insist? Well, I do insist. So that's sorted. This weekend. I'll let you know when and where later.'

Back at his flat, Jonathan prowled around restlessly. What was it about Rose that had got under his skin? Okay, so she was beautiful, but God knew he had dated beautiful women before. Even a supermodel. No, it wasn't that. It was her. That dogged air of determination mixed with an underlying vulnerability and genuineness that he had never come across before. She wasn't the least bit interested in his title or his wealth. She wasn't bowled over by him the way most women were. In fact, she gave the distinct impression she was unimpressed by him, almost disapproving.

That probably hit the nail on the head. She probably thought he didn't have a serious, committed bone in his body. And what was wrong with that? Wasn't it important to have fun in life? There would be plenty time for settling down in the future. A shiver of revulsion ran through him. The words 'settling down' and 'Jonathan Cavendish' didn't really go in the same sentence. Hell, he just had to look at his father and his serial marriages to know what a waste of time getting married was. He had a damn cheek to accuse him of a lack of commitment and responsibility. Look at the way he had treated his mother. She had hardly been cold before he had taken up with some one new. What kind of recommendation for married life was that?

But Rose was different. He suspected when she gave her heart, it would be for keeps. And the man she gave it to would have to be deserving. She was a challenge. That was it. That was the true reason he was attracted to her. Never before had he been turned down by a woman and it wasn't going to happen now. He would take her on the kind of date that she would like. Something that would convince her that he saw her for who she was and not just another woman. It was obvious that parties on yachts weren't for her. What did she say she liked? Being outdoors. Long walks, sitting in with a book when it was raining outside. Playing her guitar. What else? Picnicking.

He had gone about trying to impress her the wrong way. When they went for their date, he would show her he was sensitive and thoughtful and that he didn't need wild parties or crowds of people. He sat down on a chair by the window and looked out at the lights of London below. An idea was beginning to form in his head. He thought he knew exactly where to take her. Somewhere she would get to know the real Jonathan Cavendish.

CHAPTER EIGHT

JONATHAN collected Rose, as promised, on Saturday morning. He came in and spent a few minutes making small talk with her parents, accepting a cup of coffee from Rose's mother and engaging her father in a dissection of the latest football results.

'Just let me know when you fancy going to another match. I can always get tickets.' He paused. 'I don't suppose you're a cricket fan, are you? I've a couple of tickets for Lords next weekend.'

Rose suppressed a groan. If anything, her father preferred cricket to football. If the two of them started talking cricket, goodness knew when it would stop. She was delighted in her father's improvement. Managing at the football match had given him a lift. Every day he was more like the man he had been before the stroke and for that alone she could have kissed Jonathan.

'Now, you two. That's enough talk about cricket. Shouldn't you and Rose be getting on your way?' Rose's mother stepped in.

Jonathan rose to his feet. 'You know my flat actually overlooks Lords. Why don't you come to lunch the next time there's a match on? We get a great view from the drawing-room window.'

Rose's father slid a glance at his daughter. She knew he would love to go, but didn't want to agree without knowing how his daughter felt about it.

'It's up to you, Dad,' she said. But she gave him a small shake of her head. She really didn't want to be any more beholden to Jonathan than they already were. Despite her best intentions, they were being drawn increasingly into Jonathan's life, and she had to remember that no good could come of it.

'One day perhaps, son,' Rose's father answered.

'Any time, at all. Just let Rose know.' Jonathan jumped to his feet. 'I'll have your daughter back before it gets too late.'

She was back in a time warp. Get her home before it gets too late indeed. Who did he think she was? Cinderella?

'Don't wait up, Mum, Dad. It's just possible I'll go the pub and catch up with the gang when we get back.' Put that in your pipe and smoke it, she thought, pleased that she had made the point. She would decide when she came home. Not him.

'Where are we going?' Rose asked as they sped up the motorway, heading north. She hadn't known what to wear. He could be taking her anywhere, another party, lunch with some of his friends, anywhere. Not knowing, she had decided on a simple summer dress, hoping that it would see her through most eventualities. Her glasses were back in place as, try as she would, she still didn't quite have the hang of the contact lenses. But at least with her glasses she could see, and with her hair tied back in its usual plait, she felt collected and in control.

'You'll have to wait and see,' Jonathan said obliquely. 'I had the damnedest time trying to decide where to take you, but I hope I've got it right.'

'As long as I'm appropriately dressed, I don't care.'

'You would be appropriately dressed even if you wore a sack,' Jonathan replied.

Huh. More of his empty compliments. If she wore a sack, she would look like a bag lady. Who was he trying to kid? On the other hand, Jonathan would look perfectly at home where ever they went. Even in the faded jeans and open-necked, short-sleeved shirt he was wearing. A lock of hair flopped across his forehead and he kept brushing it away as he drove.

After an hour he turned off the motorway and onto a road bordered by fields which, in turn, gave way to a smattering of houses. A sign welcomed them to Cambridge.

'I don't know if this was the right place to take you,' he said. 'But I thought we could hire a punt and stop along the bank for a picnic. I used to do that regularly when I was a student here and I know just the place where we can tie up the boat.'

He looks nervous, Rose thought, her heart melting. She liked this more vulnerable side to him.

'Just as well it's not bucketing with rain, then.' She smiled to let him know she was teasing. 'Isn't this pretty close to where you live?'

'Yes. Cavendish House is just over half an hour to the west. And don't worry, if it had rained, I would have come up with another plan.'

'And the picnic? Did you make it yourself?'

He shook his head, looking sheepish. 'I had it delivered from Harrods.' Then they both laughed. 'Sorry, I guess old habits die hard. But, honestly, Rose, I don't think you would have found anything I made edible.'

He parked the car close to the river, near the town centre. Rose was curious. She knew little about Cambridge other than that it was a famous university town and people punted on the river. 'Show me the college you went to,' she said. She really wanted to know more about him.

He looked perplexed. 'Are you sure you're interested? They all look pretty much the same really.'

'Not to me they don't. I'd love to see where Newton, Darwin and Wordsworth lived and worked. And all the others. Go on. Indulge me.'

He bowed from the waist. 'Your wish is my command. Come on, then. I went to Trinity. In fact, we can hire a punt from there. It's in the main street. Let's see if the porters remember me. They might even let me have a look at the room I was in.' He looked pleased, Rose thought. As if he wasn't used to anyone taking an interest.

He took her by the hand and led her down streets, past several modern buildings and ancient colleges. Rose kept swivelling her head to look at buildings, a round church, a medieval house, but Jonathan propelled her on.

'I want to show you the Bridge of Sighs first,' he said. He was like an excited schoolboy and Rose warmed to this new side of him. He was constantly challenging her preconceptions of him.

'It connects the older part of St John's College to the newer part.' He pulled her through heavy wooden gates, past the porter's lodge and into a courtyard. Rose stopped in her tracks. Elegant buildings with intricate stained-glass windows looked down from every side. Students scurried about chatting, books under their arms, oblivious to their surroundings.

'Wow,' she breathed. 'I think if I came here to study I'd never get any work done. I'd just want to sit and take in my surroundings.'

Jonathan looked at her strangely. 'I suppose it is magnificent,' he said. 'I guess I stopped seeing it after a while.' His mouth turned up at the corners in the way that always made her knees go weak. 'I love seeing it all through your eyes. It's like I never really saw it before.'

Rose's heart squeezed. Why did he keep saying those things? Making her believe he could love her?

'Come on,' he said. 'It gets better.' He led her through another archway that led onto a covered bridge. The stone bridge was intricately carved. Someone must have spent years working on it. Her father would love to see it, as only one artisan could really appreciate the work of another.

'I can see why it's called the Bridge of Sighs,' Rose said. 'It's so beautiful, you just want to sigh with pleasure when you see it.'

'It's named after the Bridge of Sighs in Venice,' Jonathan told her. 'People think it's a copy but, apart from the romanticism of the two bridges, all they have in common is that they are both covered.'

'Hey, don't spoil it for me. Imagine being able to do that.' Rose half smiled. 'I love that so

I'll have one built just like it where I live.' She turned to Jonathan. 'That's the kind of world you live in,' she said softly. 'Where money and position makes anything possible.'

'You don't approve?'

'I don't approve or disapprove. I just can't imagine ever being in that position.' And that was the truth. Her world and Jonathan's were miles apart. They could have come from different planets for all they had in common.

'We're not so different, really, you and I, Rose.' Jonathan lifted his hand and tipped her chin until she was looking directly in his eyes.

Strange feelings were fizzing around inside Rose, making her breathless. What was he doing? Was he *trying* to make her fall in love with him? Didn't he know he had already succeeded? She pulled away, putting distance between them. If she stayed near him, she knew she wouldn't be able to stop herself from winding her arms around his neck.

'So where's the college you went to? What did you say it was called?'

'Trinity. We can get to it this way.' He took her hand again and led her towards a building covered in what looked like ivy, but which was what Jonathan told her was Virginia creeper. He pointed upwards. 'My last room was up there. It had a view of the river. Come and see the chapel.'

The chapel was breathtaking with its high arched ceilings and stained-glass windows. Pews lined either side, with a candle at each seat. Rose could imagine evening service, especially in the winter with the snow lying thickly outside and the music of the choir in the soft candlelight. She could appreciate the history in every stone, every worn flagstone and see, in her mind's eye, the centuries of scholars who had walked down the aisle before her.

'Seen enough?' Jonathan said quietly. He had been standing behind her, watching her closely.

She nodded. The more she knew about Jonathan the more she knew how much she wished things could have been different. The Jonathan she was learning about was someone she could imagine a future with. If she had one. The knowledge that soon she would be leaving, probably never to see him again, was tearing her up inside.

'If you want to look around some more, I'll

just get the picnic from the car. When you've seen enough, wait for me down by the river. I'll only be a few minutes.'

Rose wandered around, torn up inside. In this chapel she could let herself hope that somehow everything would work out fine and that some kind of miracle would happen, freeing her from the threat of death hanging over her, giving her back her future. But she couldn't let herself think like that. Even if this thing inside her head never changed, even if she lived a long time, she still couldn't ever risk having children.

Pain lanced through her. She would have loved babies. Two, maybe three. Why did life have to be so unfair? She shook her head, angrily brushing away the tears that stung her eyes. There was no point in feeling sorry for herself. She had to stay positive. Back in Edinburgh she had a job she loved, many friends and her music. It was entirely possible that she would have many years in front of her to enjoy life. That would have to be enough. She would *make* it enough. Even if it was to be a life without children—or Jonathan.

By the time she made her way down to the river bank, she had managed to get her emotions back under control and when Jonathan appeared with the picnic basket, she laughed. Grief, how many did he think he was catering for? She couldn't help but look past him, half expecting a stream of his friends to be following close behind. But, no, it seemed as if it really was just the two of them.

'What on earth have you got in there? A kitchen sink? The kitchen?'

'I don't know, but it's damned heavy. They kept on asking me what I wanted and I didn't have a clue, so I said yes to everything. They did say there was wine, plates, a tablecloth. For all I know, they've stuck a set of tables and chairs in there while they were at it.'

'As long as the weight doesn't sink us.'

'Nope, we should be fine.' He lugged the basket down to the bank of the river. After a few words with the person hiring out the punts Jonathan jumped into one and set the basket down. He then helped Rose into the boat. She was delighted to find that her seat was padded and comfortable. She sat back, trailing her hand in the water as Jonathan balanced on the other end of the punt, using the long pole to push away from the side of the river.

Rose closed her eyes, letting the sun warm her face and allowing the gentle splash of water as Jonathan pushed them along to soothe her. They passed under overhanging trees of willows, their long branches reaching into the river. Rose was pleasantly surprised. This was exactly the kind of day out she loved. Jonathan had got it exactly right. It seemed she was always having to reassess her opinion of him. And the more she found out about him, the deeper she fell in love. Her heart contracted with the pain of it. How was she going to find the strength to leave him when the time came? She pushed the thought away, not wanting to spoil another moment of whatever time she had left with him.

'Aren't you going to serenade me?' she asked, looking at him through slitted eyes. 'Isn't that a necessary part of the deal?'

'You obviously haven't heard me sing, or you wouldn't be suggesting it.' He grinned back. 'But you can sing well enough for both of us.'

She shook her head sleepily. 'I can't sing without my guitar. Don't know why. Maybe it's because it gives me something to hide behind.'

As soon as the words were out, she could have bitten her tongue.

Jonathan looked at her curiously. 'Why would you want to hide? Do you truly not know how beautiful you are?'

Rose snorted. 'Nice try, Jonathan, but save the compliments for someone who believes them.'

'Has anyone ever told you that you are the most exasperating woman? Or that when someone gives you a compliment, a sincere compliment, you should accept it with good grace?'

'In which case, thank you, kind sir. And has anyone ever told you that you have a fine punting action?'

Jonathan laughed and passed a hand across his forehead. 'It's much warmer than I thought it would be. Would you mind if I took my shirt off?'

Ever the gentleman. All the men of Rose's acquaintance would have removed their shirts whenever they felt like it. But as Jonathan shrugged out of his, she bit down on her lip. Maybe she should have insisted he keep it on. Now she was going to have to keep her eyes averted from his chest lest he read some of the thoughts that were going through her head. She smiled. A man like Jonathan probably had a very good idea of was going through her mind.

'Would you like to try?' he asked. 'It's really very easy.'

'Sure,' Rose said.

'Okay, come over to where I am.'

Rose picked her way to the stern of the boat, where Jonathan was standing. As she came alongside him, the boat wobbled. In a flash Jonathan wrapped his arm around her waist to steady her. A tingling sensation started in her waist and was soon fizzing around her body. Just for a second she let herself breath in heady scent of his aftershave mixed with the masculine smell of his sweat. Then he released her gently.

'Stand with your legs slightly apart for balance. Then you push the pole all the way down until it touches the bottom. Push hard then pull it all the way up. No, that's not enough.' His hands were on hers, guiding them, and she could feel the heat of his body as he stood behind her. It was making her flustered. 'You have to pull the pole through your hands until you're almost gripping the bottom. And if you want to steer, you push the pole, when it's in the water, to the left or the right. Got it?'

It was much more difficult than Jonathan had made it look. The pole was heavy, unwieldy and Rose was glad Jonathan stayed where he was to help her. Nevertheless, she was determined to do it on her own, and after a little while she got into a rhythm.

'I can manage by myself from here on,' she told Jonathan. 'You sit down.'

'Er, are you sure? It can be hard work.'

She turned to look into his face. 'I can do this. Now, scoot. Go and relax.'

Okay, so their progress wasn't quite as smooth as it had been. The punt had a disconcerting habit of weaving from one side of the river bank to another, almost as if the damn thing had a life of its own, but at least she hadn't crashed it, and they were heading in the right general direction.

'The bridge we're passing under now is called the mathematical bridge,' Jonathan said. Rose allowed herself a quick glance up and away from what she was doing. The bridge was an odd-looking wooden affair, as if a child had taken giant wooden Meccano and stuck it all together. It didn't look very mathematical.

'Why do they call it that?'

'I'm not absolutely sure. Rumour has it that it was originally put together without nuts and bolts and a mathematician at one of the colleges wanted to know how it was done. So he pulled it apart. Only he couldn't get it to go back together without nuts and bolts.'

Rose peered at the bridge again, trying to see better. But with her attention distracted, she suddenly realised that she had forgotten to lift the pole from the water and it was now behind her. Panicking lest she drop the pole into the river, she held on for dear life. But all that happened was that she was pulled out of the punt and into the water.

She shrieked as she was submerged in water the colour of pea soup. Disoriented, she bobbed to the surface, gasping.

Jonathan had retrieved an oar from the bottom of the punt and was making his way back to her.

'You should have told me you fancied a swim,' he said, reaching an arm out to her. 'I would have found a better place.'

Rose was mortified and scowled when she saw the broad grin on his face.

She grabbed his hand and found herself unceremoniously hauled back into the punt where she lay gasping like a fish that had just been landed.

'Are you okay?' Jonathan had lost the smile and was looking concerned. But Rose could have sworn there was a hint of laughter in his words.

'Apart from the fact I feel like a prize idiot and that I'm soaked, yes, I'm fine. You could even say I've never been better.' She glared at him, but then despite herself she had to laugh. It hadn't been Jonathan's fault and from his point of view it must have been funny.

Jonathan retrieved the pole from the water.

'Shall we go back?'

'I'd rather get dried out first. I don't fancy having to walk through Cambridge town centre like this.'

'The place I was going to stop is just a little further.'

A few metres on and Rose was being helped out of the punt onto dry land. Jonathan heaved the picnic basket on shore and opened it. He pulled out a white linen tablecloth.

'Take this,' he said 'Remove your wet things and wrap this around you.' He pointed to some trees. 'There's a little hollow over there. You can't be seen unless someone actually stands over you. Your things will dry out in the sun.'

It was getting worse and worse. But Rose knew the sensible thing was to do as he suggested. The alternative, waiting for her clothes to dry while she was actually in them, wasn't really an option. She would freeze.

In the relative privacy of the hollow, she slipped out of her sundress. Leaving on her bra and pants, she wrapped the sheet around her toga style. Making sure the ends were firmly tucked in, she laid her dress on the grass to dry. At least she had taken her shoes off when she had first stepped on to the punt, otherwise they'd be ruined.

By the time she returned, Jonathan had emptied the picnic basket. He raised an eye at her unconventional outfit before opening a Thermos flask and pouring a cup of steaming-hot coffee.

'Here, this will warm you up.' Then he laughed. 'You look like a Greek goddess in that get-up.'

Rose squirmed with embarrassment under his gaze. Greek goddess, her foot. More like a drowned rat, she would have thought.

He handed her his shirt. 'Put this round your shoulders. It will help keep you warm.'

Rose shrugged into the shirt, which smelled faintly of him. It came to just above her knees and realising it would cover the essentials she slithered out of the tablecloth. Now she felt almost normal again. She used the tablecloth to blot the worst of the river from her hair.

'So much for the tablecloth, I'm afraid.' She laid it next to her dress. The sun would dry it along with her clothes.

'You're still cold.' Jonathan reached out and took her feet in his hands. He began massaging them with the pads of his thumbs. Delicious ripples ran from her feet before pooling in her belly. She tried to pull her feet away, but Jonathan held them firmly. Giving up, she relaxed, propping herself on her elbows and closing her eyes, giving in to the interesting sensations his touch was provoking. The sun emerged from the clouds, warming her face. In the distance she could hear laughter as children played and the gentle sound of the breeze through the leaves of the tree. In all her dreams she would never have imagined this scenario. She and Jonathan, just the two of them, as if they were meant to be together, for ever. If she had known, she would have run and kept on running. Fate was cruel. To show her love now, to give her a glimpse of what might have been, was so unfair.

'That's better,' Jonathan said, releasing her feet. 'Now, what about something to eat?'

Rose wasn't sure whether she could eat anything. Her mouth was as dry as dust. She nodded, not trusting herself to speak. Jonathan unpacked the basket, laying out a bottle of wine, glasses, china plates and cutlery. Next came the food. There were tiny quiches, olives, crusty bread, cheese, cold meats. As Rose had suspected, there was enough to feed an army. Her mouth began to water. It had been a long time since breakfast.

Jonathan lifted an olive. 'You like?' he asked with a quirk of his lips. Rose nodded.

He held the olive to her lips. Her eyes looked

into his and her breath stopped in her throat as her chest tightened. Involuntarily her lips parted and he popped the olive into her mouth. He watched as she chewed slowly, never taking his eyes off her. Rose's heart was beating like a pneumatic drill and she couldn't believe he didn't hear it. He trailed a finger across her lips, catching a slick of olive oil. Then slowly, ever so slowly, he leaned forward and placed his mouth gently on hers. Her head swam as she tasted him. The firm pressure of his mouth. His tongue flicking across hers. He groaned and pulled her into his arms where she rested between his long legs. His kisses grew more demanding. Rose gave in to the sensations coursing through her body, returning kiss for kiss. Letting her hands drift behind his head to pull him closer, revelling in the taste of him, the warmth of his skin, the solid strength of his muscles.

He trailed a hand across her neck, sending sparks of desire coursing through her. His hand slipped under the shirt she was wearing, searching, caressing her skin until she thought she would go mad with her need from him.

They lay down, stretching their bodies along each other, straining to meet along their whole length. She could feel the hardness of his desire for her against her hips and she shifted her body so that she fitted against him perfectly.

'I've never met anyone like you,' Jonathan said eventually. 'I can't believe I've lived almost thirty years without meeting you. I think I've been looking for you all my life.'

A cold breeze fluttered down Rose's spine. This wasn't supposed to happen. She wasn't supposed to fall in love with him, or him with her. It was meant to be harmless fun. No broken hearts on either side. A few more days, then she'd be out of his life for good. The sun vanished behind a cloud. She shivered.

'You're cold,' Jonathan said. He reached out a hand and pulled her to her feet. 'Why don't we take the rest of this back to my place? I can light a fire, and we can eat the rest of the picnic in bed.' His eyes were glowing. There was no mistaking his intent. His green eyes were dark, almost pleading.

Rose knew she should run, but she also knew she couldn't. If all she had was this one night, then she had to have it. She could no more deny herself than fly to the moon.

* * *

Jonathan watched as Rose packed the food back into the basket. When he had seen her emerge from behind the tree, her damp hair in disarray, he had thought he had never seen anyone more beautiful, or more desirable. Then when she had slipped into his shirt, her long legs appearing to go for miles where his shirt skimmed her bottom, her nipples evident through the sheer fabric, she had sent his libido into overdrive. He much preferred this Rose even to the elegant woman of the fundraising dinner. Damn. He much preferred this woman to any of the sleek, polished women he had been out with over the years. What he had felt for them had been lust, pure and simple. What he felt for Rose was different. Desire, yes. So much it hit him like a punch to his solar plexus. But so much more. Tenderness. Joy in her company. Delight in seeing his world through her eyes. He reeled from the mixture of fear and excitement as he realised the truth. He loved Rose Taylor. He had been waiting for her all his life, and from now on nothing would ever be the same.

They were silent in the drive to his house. Rose kept sneaking little glances at Jonathan. The air between them sizzled with anticipation. Every time he caught her looking at him he would smile and her heart would flutter as if a hundred butterflies were trapped within her chest.

Inside his house, Jonathan closed the door and, taking her by the hand, led her to the bedroom. Kicking the bedroom door closed, he reached for her and pulled her into his arms.

'I've never wanted a woman the way I want you, Rose,' he said hoarsely.

Rose raised her face to his, knowing that whatever the next few days, weeks and months brought, she was exactly where she wanted to be for the rest of her life.

She wound her arms around his neck then his mouth was on hers and she gave herself up to him.

Much later they cuddled up in front of the fire, and finished off their picnic.

Rose leaned against his chest. His arms were wrapped around her as they watched the flickering flames.

'It won't be long before I go back,' she said quietly.

She sensed him take a deep intake of breath. 'You don't have to go. Stay with me.'

She twisted her head until she could see his face. 'I'm not talking just about tonight. I mean go back to Edinburgh. I have a life there. A home. Friends. Whatever this is, you and I know it can't last.'

'What do you mean? It can last as long as we both want it to.'

Sadness washed over her. Jonathan couldn't know that each moment could be their last. He couldn't know and, what was more, she was determined he would never know. She knew she could never hurt him like that. This thing in her brain could burst at any time. If it didn't kill her, it could leave her helpless and she would never be a burden on anyone. It scared her more than death.

'We're different, you and I,' she said softly. 'You have your life and I have mine. That's okay.'

Jonathan threw back his head and laughed. 'You think because I'm the son of a lord, because I'll inherit a title one day, that that means we can't be together. My God, Rose. This is the twenty-first century. Even princes marry who they want.'

'But we're not talking marriage, are we? We

hardly know each other.' She shook her head, forcing a laugh. 'Let's not make more of this than it is.' She turned away so she couldn't see his eyes, knowing she was hurting him.

'I know you well enough to know you are everything I ever wanted. But I don't expect you to feel the same. That's why we need time. Time for me to convince you that I'm not beyond redemption.' He smiled wryly. 'Somehow I know my partying days are behind me.' He hugged her tighter. 'Don't give up on me, Rose. Not yet.'

His hands were on her body again. She wished he wouldn't do that. How was she expected to think clearly when her head was full of him? Her body burning at his touch, her need for him so strong? But this right now was all she could offer him. All she had. She turned around and sat facing him, wrapping her legs around his hips.

'Enough talking,' she said, before pulling his face towards hers.

The next days were the most bitter-sweet of Rose's life. She burned every memory of Jonathan into her head. During the day, they would steal kisses, small touches and share glances. Then at night, after she'd been home to check up on her father, he would collect her from her parents' house and drive her back to his town house. As soon as the door closed behind them, they would be in each other's arms, tearing at each other's clothes, often not even making it to the bedroom.

On the rare occasions they didn't see other she would sit in her room, strumming her guitar, composing lyrics to new songs in her head. It was the happiest time of her life—and the saddest. Sometimes her head would ache and she would be terrified it was a sign the aneurysm was going to burst. She spent hours on the internet going over the options, but if she was hoping to find an easy solution she was disappointed. As the doctors had pointed out, there were only two. She could have surgery. Or not. Whatever she decided, the outcome could be the same. Paralysis, possibly death.

Not much of a choice, then. Do nothing and continue to live as she had been. Making the most of every day. But it was a life without a future. A day-to-day existence. A life where she wouldn't marry, have children or, worst of all, Jonathan. And the other option? Have the operation, knowing the consequences, but also knowing it offered at least a chance for a future. One where she was free to love and be loved. Have children. Grow old.

Until she had met Jonathan, doing nothing had made sense. Now she wanted more.

She paced her little room, her throat tightening as she remembered happier times. Her father strong and healthy, the house filled with love and laughter, the future still a merciful blank.

One thing she knew for certain. She couldn't tell Jonathan. He would insist on sticking by her whatever happened, and she couldn't allow that to happen. How soon would it be before his love changed to duty, regret, even loathing. Instinctively she knew he would never leave her.

Neither could she talk to him about it. He would want to help her make a decision. Then whatever she did, whatever the consequences, he would feel responsible. She loved him too much for that. No, only one person could decide what to do, and that was her.

Her aching heart told her the truth before her

brain could accept it. She would have the operation. Place her fate in the hands of the gods. She would leave Jonathan behind, convince him somehow she didn't love him, then disappear from his life and have the operation. If it was a success, she would find him again and tell him the truth. And if it wasn't? At least she had set him free to live his life. She had a week left with him. And she would make the most of every minute.

'So I'll be back next week. On Monday, if that's okay with you?' Vicki propped a hip against the desk. 'I can't believe how much better I feel now that I've stopped being sick.' She dropped a hand to the curve of her belly and Rose felt a stab of longing that almost took her breath away. Now Vicki was coming back, she no longer had an excuse to put it off. Miss Fairweather had scheduled the operation for two weeks' time. Now that she had made the decision, she had told her parents. It had been one of the worst nights of her life. But she had found comfort at last as she had cried in her mother's arms.

Vicki glanced over at Jonathan's closed door. He was seeing a patient. 'He's going to miss you. I don't suppose you are free to cover my maternity leave?'

Rose smiled wryly. Vicki had no idea how much she hoped she would be able to be in a position to do that.

'I still have my job in Edinburgh. They're expecting me back. I don't think you can count on me covering you, although...' she reached out a hand '...I'll come back and see you when the baby is born.' Rose swallowed the lump in her throat. Please, God, let her be telling the truth.

'I'm going to miss you. Hard to imagine returning to the way it was here before you and Jenny.' Vicki indicated Jenny with a nod of her head. 'I think the patients actually prefer Jenny now they're used to her. She makes them laugh.'

'Just as well, then, because Jonathan's offered her a permanent job. Mrs Smythe Jones called into see Jonathan the other day. Apparently she's decided to emigrate to New Zealand to be with her sister.'

Vicki whistled under her breath. 'I didn't think she'd ever leave. This practice has been her life for nearly forty years. She was here when Jonathan's uncle started. She wouldn't retire last year even when Jonathan assured her that the pension the company would settle on her is almost as much as her salary. She said she'd be lonely at home. I guess if she's going to stay with her sister, lack of company won't be an issue.'

The two women turned to look across at Jenny who was patiently listening to the voice on the other end of the phone, offering periodic *oh, dear*s and *poor you*. They smiled at each other. 'I gather Jenny was out at lunch when Mrs Smythe Jones came for her chat. Somehow I can't imagine her letting Jonathan employ Jenny if she had seen the hairdo.'

Over the weeks Jenny's hair had reverted to the spiky look she loved. No one had said anything. Rose had only been glad that the piercings remained at home. Even if Jonathan and his patients accepted the hair, a nose ring was bound to be a step too far.

Rose would be leaving all this behind soon, maybe forever, and the thought was breaking her heart.

CHAPTER NINE

LATER on that day they received word that Lord Hilton had died in his sleep. Rose had become fond of the couple over the last few weeks and when Jonathan broke the news she was unsurprised at how sad she felt.

Jonathan pulled her into his arms and she rested her head there. It felt so good, so safe, and she wished she could stay there for ever. With him she could face anything, except what she feared most.

'How is Lady Hilton taking it?' Rose asked. 'Should I go to her?'

'She said to tell you that she is very grateful for everything you did for them. She has friends and family around right now, but she asks if you would come to the funeral. She says Giles wanted it.'

'Of course I'll go,' Rose said softly. She looked up at him. 'You'll be there?'

'I'm always going to be there, Rose Taylor,'

Jonathan said firmly. 'Don't you know that by now?' The look of love in his eyes made her heart shatter. 'She's also asked if you could back to the house with the others after the funeral. She has something to tell you.'

Rose could hardly speak. Her throat was tight. He loved her. She knew that without doubt, even if he hadn't said the words. Little did he know they could only have these last few days to do them for the rest of their lives. She had handed in her notice in Edinburgh, effective immediately, as the operation had been scheduled for the end of the next week. But she wouldn't tell Jonathan. For his sake, she would make him believe that she wasn't in love with him, that she wanted to go back to her life in Edinburgh. It would be hard to convince him, and the thought of hurting him was tearing her apart, but for his sake she had to make him believe her. If the operation was a success she would come back to him and tell him everything. If not? At least he would be free to live his life.

That evening Jonathan came down to her local again. They had been a couple of times and Jonathan was surprised how relaxing he found the pub and how welcoming Rose's friends were. Every time they had been there, Rose had taken her guitar and sung. Every day he fell deeper in love.

Tonight she took her guitar and perched on a chair on the stage. She caught his eye across the crowded room.

'I've a new song I'd like to sing tonight,' she said softly. 'It's something I composed recently. I hope you all like it. It's called, "All my tomorrows".'

Her voice was husky as she sang directly to him. The song was about love and loss, about making the most of every moment. The last line of the chorus was 'All my tomorrows are wrapped up in you today,' and as she sang the line her voice cracked a little. Something in the way she sang the song and in the way her eyes filled as the last notes died away scared him.

When she'd finished singing, she smiled a little shakily. The room erupted as everyone clapped and cheered, but Jonathan sat stunned. If he hadn't known better, he would think she was saying goodbye.

* * *

Lord Hilton's funeral was held a couple of days later in the family church. Summer had arrived and the mourners gathered under a blazing sun. Rose tried not to think that soon a similar crowd might be gathered to say their last farewells to her. Instead, she resolutely pushed the thought away. She wasn't going to waste a moment of whatever time she had left thinking gloomy thoughts.

And Giles's funeral wasn't gloomy. It was a celebration of a remarkable man who, as it was pointed out, had stayed in love with his wife of fifty years right until the end.

Jonathan's father was there and after the burial he came up to Rose.

'It's good to see you again, my dear,' he said. 'Won't you ask Jonathan to bring you home for dinner so we can get to know each other better?'

Rose looked him directly in the eye. If anything happened to her, Jonathan would need his father. She didn't know if she could make things right between father and son, but she had to try.

'I don't know if I can persuade him,' she said softly. 'He seems to be very angry with you.'

She took a deep breath and hurried on before she lost her nerve. 'He seems to think that you don't care about him. That perhaps you never did.'

Lord Cavendish looked aghast. Whether it was because Rose had the audacity to talk to him about what he almost certainly saw as a private matter, or whether it was because he didn't want to acknowledge the way his son felt, Rose couldn't be sure.

Suddenly his expression relaxed and he smiled grimly. 'I can see why my son is so besotted with you,' he said. 'But he can't think I don't care about him. My God, he is the most important thing in my life. Why would he think otherwise?'

'Maybe because you sent him away to boarding school after his mother died? I understand he's never lived at home since.'

Lord Cavendish pulled a hand through his still dark and thick hair that was so much like his son's. 'I sent him away because I thought it was for the best,' he said stiffly. 'I was away so much on business and without his mother…' He shrugged. 'There would be no one at home to look after him.'

Rose plunged on. Out of the corner of her eye, she could see Jonathan chatting to Lady Hilton.

'He was only a child,' she said. 'And you took him away from everything he knew and loved, just when he had suffered the most devastating loss. Didn't it occur to you that he'd need his father? At least for a while?'

Jonathan's father looked even more taken aback, if that was possible. He looked into the distance. 'I met Jonathan's mother when I was a young man at university. I loved her instantly. She was like a bright star in my otherwise lonely existence. A bit like I suspect you are to Jonathan. Like you, she didn't come from aristocracy and my parents didn't approve. It was different back then. Nobody cares these days. But it didn't matter what they thought. I couldn't imagine a future without her. I would have married her even if my family had thrown me on the street.' He smiled. 'Luckily it didn't come to that. We married and had a few short years together. She was a painter, you know. I understand from Lady Hilton that you compose songs? My Clara and you were very much alike. I was working all hours setting up my businesses while she painted. I guess it made her less lonely. Then Jonathan came along and I thought she would miss me less, so I spent even more time away from home.' His eyes were bleak. 'I missed her every second, but I thought we had years together.' His voice was hoarse as if tears weren't far away.

Unable to stop herself, Rose touched him gently on the arm, wanting to let him know she understood.

'Then when Jonathan was five, my darling Clara died. I thought I'd go mad with the pain of it. Every time I looked at Jonathan I saw his mother. I couldn't bear it. I had to throw myself into work. And I had to know they were being looked after. So, yes. I sent him away. I regret it now. I hardly know my son, and it's my fault.'

'But you married again. Several times, I gather.' Rose smiled to take the sting from her words.

'I wanted what I had with Clara, but it was no use. I never found it again.' He looked directly into her eyes.

'Have you ever been in love, Rose? I mean so in love that it feels that he's the missing part of your soul?'

Rose bit hard on her lip to stop the tears. She nodded.

'Then you'll know that no one else can ever measure up, no matter how they try. Your soul remains in two bits. A chunk of you is always missing, no matter how much you search.'

'But you still have part of her. In Jonathan,' Rose said, forcing the words past her frozen throat.

She followed his gaze until it rested on Jonathan. His eyes softened. 'I know I do. But I think I may have left it too late.'

'It's never too late.' Then, at the realisation of what she'd said, she added, 'At least, it's not for you two. Talk to him. I know it's difficult. But tell him what you told me, about Clara. I think you'll find he understands.'

Lord Cavendish gave her a long appraising look. He grinned and Rose's heart skipped a beat. In that instant she could see the man Jonathan would become as he aged. What she would give to be around to see it. 'I think I'm going to like having you around, Rose Taylor,' Lord Cavendish said slowly. 'Now, if you'll excuse me, I think I should go and talk to my son.'

Rose watched as Lord Cavendish walked over to his son. He placed a hand on Jonathan's shoulder and after a few words the two men walked off together.

Later, back in the Hiltons' home, Sophia asked Rose to come into her study for a few moments. Rose was baffled. The day was taking its toll on her and she didn't know how much she could hold it all together. But if Sophia Hilton could keep a brave face even if she was breaking up inside, so could she.

Lady Hilton opened a desk drawer and pulled out an envelope. She handed it to Rose.

'Giles wanted you to have this, my dear. In the short time we've known you, we've come to look on you as a daughter.'

Intrigued, Rose opened the envelope. Inside was a cheque, the sum of which made her gasp.

'What on earth…? You can't possibly mean to give this to me. It's far too generous and completely unnecessary.'

Sophia smiled. 'It's for your wedding. Giles and I both see the way things are with you and Jonathan. We don't have daughters of our own, and it gives us both...' She drew a shaky breath. ' I mean, the thought of you using it to get married gave us so much pleasure.'

'But I'm not getting married. J-Jonathan and I haven't even s-spoken of it,' Rose stuttered.

'But you will, my dear.'

Rose thrust the envelope back at Sophia. 'I'm sorry. I really can't take this. There isn't going to be a wedding, whatever you might think.' Her throat was clogging with tears and she could barely speak.

'Don't you believe he loves you? Is that what you think? Or do you think he won't marry you because you have some misguided idea about class? But, my dear, Jonathan's mother was the same and it didn't stop his father from marrying her. And back then people did make more of it.'

It was all too much. The funeral. The Hiltons' kindness. That a couple she barely knew had been thinking of her even while going through the most horrible and sad time. Knowing that her days with Jonathan were about to come to an end. She couldn't bear it.

'I'm sorry,' she managed. 'I really have to go.' And before she could disgrace herself by breaking down completely, she fled.

CHAPTER TEN

ON WHAT was to be their last night together, although of course Jonathan had no idea that it would be, Rose suggested they spend the night at his house near Cambridge. It was where they had first made love and the place she had been happiest in all her life.

If Jonathan suspected something, he gave no sign of it. In fact, he looked as if he was up to something. There was a hidden air of excitement about him that Rose had never seen before. Her heart was cracking with the unbearable realisation that this could be the last time she would ever be in his arms.

'We can pop into to see Mary first, if you don't mind. She's back at work after her time off and I want to check she's not doing too much.'

'Of course,' Rose agreed. The doctors at the hospital had diagnosed angina but with some changes to her diet and some additional gentle exercise they were hopeful she would live for many years yet.

They found Mary ensconced in her kitchen domain. The older lady had lost a little weight and was delighted to see them.

'Jonathan and Rose! Thank you for coming to see me.' She sent Jonathan a mock severe look. 'Although how you smelled my baking all the way from London is anyone's guess.'

'Is Father here?' Jonathan asked Mary, after hugging her.

'He is. Thankfully without that woman. She seems to have been chucked. Thank God he saw sense before it was too late.' She dropped her voice. 'Why don't you go and see him? He's always talking about you, you know. Telling me how proud you make him and how very proud your mother would be.'

Jonathan smiled awkwardly.

'So he keeps telling me. This new father is taking a bit of getting used to,' he said. 'I wonder what brought about this change.' But the look he slid Rose told her he knew about their conversation, although until now, he hadn't mentioned it.

'Ah, my dear boy. It makes an old woman

happy to know that you two have made up. He loves you, you know.'

Jonathan shuffled his feet uncomfortably. 'And I him, Mary. Now, any chance of us raiding your kitchen for some food? I'm going to steal Rose away for a private dinner in my cottage.'

His look sent bitter-sweet memories ricocheting around Rose's head. More than anything she didn't want to waste a single moment that they had left.

'Can't you stay for dinner? Your father would love to have the company.'

Jonathan looked at Rose for agreement and when she nodded her head he said, 'Okay. I suppose Rose and I will have plenty other times.'

Blast Lord Cavendish and blast her interference, Rose thought briefly. But wasn't this exactly what she'd engineered? Jonathan wasn't to know this was their last night.

Dinner seemed to go on for ever, although Lord Cavendish was surprisingly amusing company. It was good to see the two men, so alike, sharing jokes and later their memories of Clara. It seemed astonishing to Rose that Jonathan knew so little about his mother. Lord Cavendish included Rose in the conversation, making it obvious that his interest in her was genuine.

Finally, when it was almost ten o'clock, dinner was over and Jonathan made their excuses.

Once inside his house, he reached out for and brought his mouth down on hers as if he were drowning and she were a life raft. Although Rose wanted nothing more than to be naked beside him in his bed, there was another memory she needed to leave him with. A memory she hoped that when she was gone he would recall and know deep down that she had loved him and her leaving hadn't been her choice. She wanted to sing to him one last time, so that one day in the future he would understand why she had acted as she had.

She disentangled herself from his arms. 'I want you to sit there and not move,' she ordered.

Bemused, Jonathan wasn't having it. 'No way. Right now I want you too much to keep my hands off you.' And then he was kissing her again and Rose was lost. She gave herself up to him greedily, wanting to burn every part of him into her soul.

Later she lay in his arms and he looked at her through half-closed lids.

'I love you, Rose,' he said huskily. 'And I'll go to my grave loving you.'

Rose's heart sang. But she couldn't say the words he longed to hear. If she did, he would never stop looking for her.

She forced a laugh. 'Wow! That's a surprise. I had no idea you felt that way.' She slipped out of bed and started to get dressed, avoiding his eyes. If he saw her eyes, she knew her anguish would be plain to see.

She sensed his puzzlement.

'Is that all you have to say?' He leapt out of bed and came to stand behind her, wrapping her in his arms. 'Don't you get it? I love you and I want to spend the rest of my life with you. I want you to do me the honour of becoming my wife, Rose.'

Rose wriggled out of his grasp. 'But I don't want to marry you. I'm sorry, Jonathan, whatever we had, whatever this was…' She indicated the unmade bed with a sweep of her hand. 'For me it was just an interlude. Some fun. I'm going back to Edinburgh. My life is there.'

'Going back? You can't. What about us? Even if you don't love me now, I know you feel something.' He pulled his hand through his hair. 'I can't be wrong. Everything tells me I'm not wrong.'

She forced herself to continue dressing.

'I'm sorry, Jonathan, I could never marry someone like you. All you're really interested in is having a good time. When I marry...' Her voice cracked and she breathed deeply, knowing how much she was hurting him. 'It will be to someone who knows that there is more to life than having fun. Someone I can respect.'

'My God, Rose, I know I'm not the kind of man you would have wished for yourself. But I love you. I can change. No more parties, I promise. I didn't tell you but I've taken a part-time job at the local hospital. I'm going to complete my surgical training. It's what I always wanted to do.'

'What about your uncle's practice?'

'I'll employ someone else to keep it on. You've made me realise that I need more in my life. What I had before I met you was meaningless. Empty.'

'You shouldn't change your whole life around because of me,' Rose said sadly, 'especially when after tonight I'm no longer going to be in it.'

She turned and looked him directly in the eye. She knew the tears would come later. But she had to hurt him now, even if it broke her heart.

'I've had a good time, Jonathan. You showed me a different side to life and I'll always be grateful to you. But it's over. I'm going back to Edinburgh and there's nothing you can do, or say, that'll make me change my mind. I don't love you and I never will.'

Jonathan's green eyes turned cool.

'You've been stringing me along all this time, haven't you?' he said bitterly. 'None of this meant anything to you, did it?' He pulled his jeans over his hips. 'Well, I can't say I haven't deserved to be taken for a ride. God knows, I've hurt others. Now it seems it's my turn.' He laughed sourly. 'And the irony of it all is that I've spent all my life not believing that it was possible to love one person for the whole of my life. Until you showed me that that was exactly how my father felt about my mother. I guess at least I have you to thank for that.'

Rose recoiled from the look in his eyes. She longed to put her arms around him and tell him the truth. But she couldn't. If she touched him, she'd be undone.

He slipped his shirt on and picked up his car keys. 'I think I should take you home now.'

CHAPTER ELEVEN

Rose lay on the hospital bed, feeling groggy. The premeds were taking the edge off her anxiety, but couldn't quite take it away. She wondered if these few minutes would be the last she would know.

'You can still change your mind,' her mother whispered. Behind the forced smile, Rose could see her terror.

Rose smiled faintly. She reached for her mother's hand. 'I've made up my mind, Mum. I'm going through with it.' Her head had been shaved where they were planning to operate. Knowing that they would do that, she had gone to the hairdresser yesterday and insisted they crop her hair. She hardly recognised herself. And not just because of the haircut. Her face was gaunt, her eyes haunted. She wondered what Jonathan would think of her new hairstyle. She closed her eyes. She could see him clearly, his smile, his eyes. She could almost taste his skin. She pushed the image away. She couldn't think of Jonathan. Not now. If she did she might not have the strength to go through with it; she might just persuade herself that whatever days she had left were better spent with him. But she knew she could never risk breaking his heart.

'Please let me call him.' It was as if her mother could read her mind. She had begged Rose to let Jonathan know, but Rose had held steadfast. Instead, she had written the words to the song she had written for him, and asked her mother to give it to him should anything happen to her. Her father was at home, refusing to say what might be his last goodbyes to his only child. His doctor had advised him against coming to the hospital earlier, worried that the added strain would set him back.

'I'll be there when you wake up,' he had said before she left for the hospital. He had held her and kissed her hair, murmuring words that she remembered from her childhood.

'We've been through this, Mum, and you promised.' Rose squeezed her mother's hand. 'And if something happens to me, if I survive the operation but am brain damaged, remember you swore you won't tell him. I'd rather he remembered me how I was.'

'But...' her mother smiled weakly, '...you're going to be fine. Everything is going to be just fine.'

All too soon, they came to take her to Theatre. Rose could hardly bear the pain in her mother's eyes as they kissed for what could be the last time. Then she was in Theatre and the anaesthetist was asking her to count backwards from a hundred. Now she allowed herself to think of Jonathan. To bring his dear face into her mind, and as she drifted off, she imagined his lips on hers.

Jonathan was restless. Since Rose had left him, nothing could distract him from the thoughts and memories of her. He couldn't bring himself to attend any of the parties or lunches to which he still got invited. All he wanted was Rose. The only thing that kept him sane were his patients and his work. If it hadn't been for them he would have gone stark, staring mad. Several times, more often than he cared to count, he had considered jumping on a plane to Edinburgh to go searching for her. Maybe he could still persuade her to come back to him. He just couldn't believe she didn't love him, even a little bit.

Picking up his car keys, he made up his mind. He would call in on her parents. See how her father was doing. Maybe he could get an address out of them. At the very least, he could be where she lived. If he couldn't be with her, being where she was until recently would be the next best thing.

Half an hour later, he rang the doorbell. A taxi pulled up behind his car. After a long pause Rose's father came to the door. He was still leaning on his stick, but Jonathan was pleased to see he seemed to hardly need it. The droop to the side of his mouth had also improved. All in all he appeared to be making a good recovery. But it was the look in his eyes that shocked Jonathan. Never before had he seen him look so sad, or so frightened, not even when he had first met him.

'What is it?' Jonathan asked. 'Is something wrong?' His heart was pounding like a runaway train. Had something happened to Rose? Please, God, no.

Tommy shook his head despairingly. 'I'm

sorry, Jonathan, I can't talk to you at the moment. My taxi's waiting for me.'

'Where's Rose's mother? Why isn't she here? Something's wrong. Is it Rose?' He blocked Tommy's path. He had to know.

'Please, Jonathan, I don't have time for this. I need to get to the hospital.'

'The hospital?' His alarm was growing stronger. There was no way that Rose's mother would let Tommy go by himself. There was something wrong. He knew it. It took every ounce of his strength not to shake the fragile man in front of him. Tommy looked at him steadily. 'She made us promise not to tell you. I think she was wrong, but I promised her.'

'Just tell me where she is.'

'I can't. I need to get to the hospital, but if you were to follow the taxi there, I couldn't stop you, could I?'

Jonathan read the message in his eyes. It was all he was going to get and it would have to do. But as he followed the painfully slow taxi through the thick London traffic, his mind was whirling with images he couldn't bear. His Rose. Dead or dying. Here in London. Why had she told them not to tell him? He didn't care. All he wanted was to know that she was all right. If he knew that, he could live the rest of his life without her. As long as he knew she was in it somewhere.

His fear almost threatened to crush him as the taxi pulled up outside the London Hospital for Neurological Sciences. Little clicks were going on inside his head. The sadness in her eyes. Her refusal to talk about the future. That song she had composed. What had the last line been? *All my tomorrows are wrapped up in you today.* What hadn't she been telling him?

Fear clutching his throat, he abandoned his car on a double yellow line—he couldn't care less if he never saw it again—and caught up with Tommy. He placed his hand under his elbow.

'She's here, isn't she?' he said flatly.

Tommy simply nodded. Something squeezed Jonathan's chest when he saw tears glisten in Tommy's eyes.

'Is she alive? Please, you have to tell me that.'

'I don't know,' Tommy said slowly. 'She's in Theatre, having an operation for a brain aneurysm. It seems it's the same thing that caused my stroke. The doctors knew it was the heredi-

tary kind, so they screened her for it.' His voice
cracked.

'And they found something?' Jonathan could
hardly breathe. It all made sense now. Terrible,
heart-breaking sense.

'She's being operated on today. I'm here to
sit with her mother and wait. We don't know
if she'll survive the operation.'

'Survive?' he could hardly force the words
past his clenched jaw. 'Of course she's going to
survive.' But try as he may, he couldn't completely remove the fear from his voice. 'It's Rose
we're talking about. And the woman I know is
a fighter.'

When Rose opened her eyes she thought she
was dreaming. Either that, or she had died and
she was in heaven. But as soon as he spoke, she
knew this was no dream and that she was very
much alive.

'Hey, how're you feeling?' His eyes looked
different somehow. Almost damp. As if he'd
being crying. Which was ridiculous. Jonathan
didn't cry.

'I'm alive?' The words were all she could
manage. A vague memory of her parents'

faces, their eyes bright with tears, swam into her head.

Jonathan slipped a hand under her shoulders and helped her take a sip of cold water. It tasted like nectar. She was alive and she could hardly believe it.

'The operation went well. Even better than the surgeon hoped. You are going to be fine. You have to take it easy for a while, but after that you can do whatever you want.'

She still couldn't quite believe what he was telling her. She wriggled her toes. That was good. Then she stretched her fingers. Movement there too. She could move, she could speak, she could see and she could understand.

Her eyes were growing heavy. 'You found me,' she whispered, before she let herself give in to sleep.

He was still there when she opened them again. He was watching her, as if he couldn't bear to tear his eyes away from her.

'Hello, love.' Her mother's voice came from the other side of the bed. Beside her was her father. They were smiling and holding hands. Her mother stood and kissed her on the cheek. 'Welcome back to us.' She stood back and let

Tommy come closer. Rose watched a fat tear slide down his cheek. Rose had never seen her father cry before and her heart ached for him.

'My child,' he said simply. 'My baby girl. You are going to have a long and happy life. Thank God.'

'We're going to leave you two alone for a few minutes,' her mother said. 'Jonathan refuses to go home until he's sure you're okay.'

She swivelled her head to look at him. His face was grey and he was unshaven. How long had he been here? Had she imagined seeing him earlier when she'd first come round?

'Don't try to speak,' he said. 'You've been sedated since the operation and you need time to rest.'

'How long?' she whispered.

'Two days. Two of the longest, hardest, scariest days of my life. How much worse for you and your parents to have lived with this for all these weeks.'

He touched her cheek with his finger. 'You need to sleep now. But when you wake up, I'll still be here. I'm never going to leave your side again.' He smiled sadly. 'No matter what you say. You're stuck with me.'

CHAPTER TWELVE

THE day was bright with promise. The sun shining just for them as Rose walked down the flower-edged path towards Jonathan. Her parents were sitting in the front row. Apart from a slight droop to the side of his mouth and a residual limp, her father had made an almost complete recovery. These days he was forever telling whoever would listen that his stroke had been the best thing that ever happened to him. After all, if it hadn't happened, Rose would never have discovered she had inherited the condition. He never finished the sentence, and he didn't need to. If her condition hadn't been discovered, if the aneurysm hadn't been removed, it was possible she might not be here. Not walking down the aisle to the man who in a few minutes would become her husband.

Instead of the traditional wedding march, a band was playing the song she had written for Jonathan. 'All my tomorrows are wrapped up in you today.' Rose's heart soared. She and Jonathan had many, many tomorrows in store for them. She still wasn't sure how she felt about being the future Lady Cavendish, but what did anything matter when she had Jonathan by her side? And he had promised it wouldn't change a thing—except perhaps end his party days. And that, he said, was no loss at all. He had everything he'd ever dreamed of. With the possible exception of four or five children. And they both agreed it would be fun making their babies.

She finished her walk up the aisle and as Jonathan looked at her, she caught her breath. She knew without a shadow of doubt that he loved her more than she'd ever thought it possible to be loved.

Holding her hand, his voice ringing out, he repeated the words from the Bible.

'"Do not urge me to leave you or turn back from following you; for where you go, I will go, and where you lodge, I will lodge. Your people shall be my people, and your God my God."' He touched her lips with his.

'Remember that, my darling. No matter what, you must never ever shut me out again. Do you promise me?' His voice was urgent, the pain of the days when he had thought he would lose her still evident in his voice.

Rose grinned at him. 'Are you kidding? You and I are stuck with each other. For better for worse, for richer, for poorer. In sickness and in health. And I for one am going nowhere. Not ever.' Happiness bubbled up inside her, filling her with a joy she had never known was possible. 'I'm here for all your tomorrows. I promise.'

MEDICAL™

Large Print

Titles for the next six months...

March

DATING THE MILLIONAIRE DOCTOR	Marion Lennox
ALESSANDRO AND THE CHEERY NANNY	Amy Andrews
VALENTINO'S PREGNANCY BOMBSHELL	Amy Andrews
A KNIGHT FOR NURSE HART	Laura Iding
A NURSE TO TAME THE PLAYBOY	Maggie Kingsley
VILLAGE MIDWIFE, BLUSHING BRIDE	Gill Sanderson

April

BACHELOR OF THE BABY WARD	Meredith Webber
FAIRYTALE ON THE CHILDREN'S WARD	Meredith Webber
PLAYBOY UNDER THE MISTLETOE	Joanna Neil
OFFICER, SURGEON...GENTLEMAN!	Janice Lynn
MIDWIFE IN THE FAMILY WAY	Fiona McArthur
THEIR MARRIAGE MIRACLE	Sue MacKay

May

DR ZINETTI'S SNOWKISSED BRIDE	Sarah Morgan
THE CHRISTMAS BABY BUMP	Lynne Marshall
CHRISTMAS IN BLUEBELL COVE	Abigail Gordon
THE VILLAGE NURSE'S HAPPY-EVER-AFTER	Abigail Gordon
THE MOST MAGICAL GIFT OF ALL	Fiona Lowe
CHRISTMAS MIRACLE: A FAMILY	Dianne Drake

MILLS & BOON™

MEDICAL™

Large Print

June

ST PIRAN'S: THE WEDDING OF THE YEAR	Caroline Anderson
ST PIRAN'S: RESCUING PREGNANT CINDERELLA	Carol Marinelli
A CHRISTMAS KNIGHT	Kate Hardy
THE NURSE WHO SAVED CHRISTMAS	Janice Lynn
THE MIDWIFE'S CHRISTMAS MIRACLE	Jennifer Taylor
THE DOCTOR'S SOCIETY SWEETHEART	Lucy Clark

July

SHEIKH, CHILDREN'S DOCTOR...HUSBAND	Meredith Webber
SIX-WEEK MARRIAGE MIRACLE	Jessica Matthews
RESCUED BY THE DREAMY DOC	Amy Andrews
NAVY OFFICER TO FAMILY MAN	Emily Forbes
ST PIRAN'S: ITALIAN SURGEON, FORBIDDEN BRIDE	Margaret McDonagh
THE BABY WHO STOLE THE DOCTOR'S HEART	Dianne Drake

August

CEDAR BLUFF'S MOST ELIGIBLE BACHELOR	Laura Iding
DOCTOR: DIAMOND IN THE ROUGH	Lucy Clark
BECOMING DR BELLINI'S BRIDE	Joanna Neil
MIDWIFE, MOTHER...ITALIAN'S WIFE	Fiona McArthur
ST PIRAN'S: DAREDEVIL, DOCTOR...DAD!	Anne Fraser
SINGLE DAD'S TRIPLE TROUBLE	Fiona Lowe